**FEARS
NO
MAN**

Additional books by Tom V. Whatley from Sunstone Press.

Cuts No Slack

He Ain't Dead

Ghost Runner

Twice As Good

The Gatekeeper

FEARS NO MAN

A Novel

Tom V. Whatley

SUNSTONE
PRESS

SANTA FE

Book and cover design by Vicki Ahl

Cover photograph by Stacy Whatley Holder

Sunstone books may be purchased for educational, business, or sales
promotional use. For information please write: Special Markets Department,
Sunstone Press, P.O. Box 2321, Santa Fe, New Mexico 87504-2321.

Library of Congress Cataloging-in-Publication Data

Whatley, Tom V., 1940-
  Fears no man : a novel / by Tom V. Whatley.
    p. cm.
  ISBN 978-0-86534-580-5 (softcover : alk. paper)
  1. Cherokee Indians--Fiction. I. Title.

PS3573.H33F43 2007
813'.54--dc22

                                        2007002182

WWW.SUNSTONEPRESS.COM
SUNSTONE PRESS / POST OFFICE BOX 2321 / SANTA FE, NM 87504-2321 /USA
(505) 988-4418 / ORDERS ONLY (800) 243-5644 / FAX (505) 988-1025

For Roslyn, my No-qui-si for forty-five years.

1

Somewhere in northern Georgia. The year was 1838.

The noon meal was finished. Franklin Adair and his two sons walked outside to continue their day's work. Suddenly a clamoring rush of horsemen filled the yard. The riders were a mixture of federal soldiers and Georgia militia. The three Adairs were surrounded immediately. Two of the soldiers jumped off their horses and ran into the house.

"There's a woman in the bed and a girl looking after her," one of the soldiers shouted.

"Drag em on out," their leader said. "We ain't got no time to nursemaid no injun."

The two men came out of the house, forcibly pushing the girl and frail woman before them.

"Hey, that young squaw looks mighty good," one of the horsemen said.

"You leave her alone," the leader said, somewhat of a humane gesture in the midst of a totally inhumane circumstance. "We ain't here for that and I won't stand for it."

"Aw, come on Sergeant. We might as well get her now as later," the man said as he laughed.

"You do and I'll see you horse whipped. Now ya'll move em on down the road to where they're holding the others. Put the woman on one of the wagons when you get there."

The soldiers moved out, forcing their captives to walk in the midst of their horses. Franklin and the two boys helped the woman along. A short distance down the road they passed three wagons. The men on the wagons were waiting for them to leave so they could pillage the belongings of the Indians. They were no more than scavengers. They would take everything of value and probably share their profit with the soldiers.

When they came to the main road they added their new captives to the thirty or so already in tow. A few of the feeble and sick were riding in wagons. The entire lot had the look of a beaten people. Without waiting, the soldiers pushed them out down the road. It was the beginning of a long journey. Many of the Cherokee nation would not survive. Long before anyone called it the Trail of Tears, those who walked it knew it was a trail of shame.

2

I was headed west. I crossed the northern part of Georgia riding the high trails and crossed the Chatooga river near it's birthplace. It was a small stream here. I then followed the river on its flow south until it ran into the Coosa. I turned west and went up a good sized mountain and onto a plateau. I stopped at the top to look over my back trail. I saw no signs of life or anybody following me. From the high ground I could see a scattering of houses and barns spread out over a long valley. The plateau took me two days of riding. I came down to the big river called the Tennessee at a place known as Gunter's landing. I then rode away from the river a good distance and followed it's direction west. I knew of the trail I followed from Agigage Wah-ya. He talked of it often and said he had traveled it many times. He spoke of the beauty of the land known as Alabama and told me we had relatives there until the Cherokee conceded the land to the government. I indeed had ridden through some of the most beautiful forests and valleys I had ever seen. The ground where I rode was flat and I preferred traveling there instead of fighting the thick brush and hilly country to the north. I rode with all the belongings I had in the world atop my packhorse. The weather was warm, but a cold breeze in my mind caused every hair on my body to bristle.

The cold wind blowing in my mind was not the winter wind. It was the bitter wind of lies and broken promises. A once proud people were now reduced to nothing more than animals. The Cherokee nation was being forcibly moved from their homeland to some far away place. Their sparkling streams and rivers were far behind. Their mountains would no longer speak to them the music of greatness. Theirs would be an existence of shame and hopelessness.

Not me. I am Tse-quo-ni, Cherokee warrior of the high mountains where the sun appears.

I had been hearing the sound for a while. It was strange, unlike anything I had ever heard. I knew the river called Tennessee was close again. I had been seeing in the distance the thick trees and green brush surrounding it rising up on the otherwise flat and open land. The sound drew me toward the river. I had to see what was making it. I tied the big black and my packhorse in a patch of grass just inside the trees along the river. The horses were happy to have the grass and I was happy to be out of the saddle.

The noise was getting louder as I belly crawled into the thick brush lining the river's edge. I had a clear view of the big river. I saw the beast making the foreign sound. It came around a bend in the river, heading in my direction. It was coughing an awful sound and belching black smoke from a pipe stuck up in the air. Wheels turned in the water on both sides. The swirling smoke masked my view at times as it engulfed the entire boat. As it came closer, I noticed four flat boats lashed together and tailing the boat making all the noise. My heart grew sick as the evil snake came by me. I saw men, women, and children of the once great Cherokee nation huddled together on the flat boats.

I could see their faces. They wore the look of defeat. I looked for familiar faces. I saw none. My mother and sister could be on these boats, I thought. Perhaps they were on the far side out of my view.

The thought occurred to me to take my rifle and shoot the soldiers guarding them. Then they could escape. Then another thought replaced it. No. The Cherokee people chose this. They forgot the old ways and accepted the ways of the white man. They trusted the white man's promises. They did not fight. They were not Cherokee.

As I lay watching the passing boats grow smaller in the distance, I remembered the story Agigage-wa-ya told me. In the white man's tongue his name was Red Wolf. One day while checking our snares we found a possum staring at us. As we approached, the possum sulled and played dead. Red Wolf used the occasion to teach me a lesson. He repeated the story often as I grew up. He asked me if I knew why the possum had no hair on it's tail.

"I do not know grandfather," I said.

"The possum once had the most beautiful tail of all the animals in the forest," he said. "It was covered with thick curly hair. The rabbit was jealous of the possum's beautiful tail. He told the possum the beauty of his tail would give him a place of high standing when the animal council met. The possum was so proud. But jealous rabbit pointed out how dirty the tail was and asked if he could help by washing it. The possum agreed. Jealous rabbit applied a special potion to the tail that would make the hair fall off. He then wrapped the tail in a snake skin and told the possum to remove it only during the meeting of the animal council or it would get dirty again. The possum did just that and removed the skin in front of all his friends to find his tail naked. The possum has lived in shame since. That is why he grins so sheepishly and plays dead. Now, can you tell me why the possum has no hair on it's tail?"

I tried to answer him but my answer did not please Red Wolf.

"It is because he trusted someone who was not worthy of trust," he exclaimed.

The truth of grandfather's story had become a part of my life. Trust no man until you are certain of his loyalty. The Cherokee people trusted the white man and now they look like the possum. They will live in shame forever. Not me. Tse-quo-ni will yield to no man. I will live and die free.

3

Tse-quo-ni went back to his horses and decided to build a small fire and spend the night where his horses could enjoy the lush grass and he could enjoy the safety of the trees around him. It was while by his fire in the night that he thought back over his past and the circumstances causing him to ride west.

Red Wolf was the first to call Tse-quo-ni by the name Soquilla-asgaya, or Horse Man. His grandfather always had horses and prided himself in them. He noticed his grandson with the horses and marveled at his natural ability to handle them. It was as if he could communicate with them. Because of his grandfather's use of the new name, many of his people called him Horse Man. He never thought much about the name. He liked it because his grandfather gave it to him but preferred the name his mother gave him. He was Rivers. His people had lived in the high mountains of North Georgia, the birth place for the great Savannah and Chattahoochee rivers. It was the place these mighty rivers played in his people's lives that caused his mother to give him his name. He enjoyed the sound of it in the Cherokee language. Tse-quo-ni. You could almost hear the music of the rivers in the word. He wore the name proudly.

His people were the Erati Tsarki. They were hunters who provided for their families by their skills with the bow and knife. He was once proud of his heritage, but the Erati Tsarki followed the ways of the Otari Tsaraki to the north and the white men who lived around them. They started planting crops. As a lad he was proud to be Erati Tsarki. Not any more. No Cherokee warrior should dig the earth like some white man.

Rivers was tall for a Cherokee. At nineteen, he stood six feet and three inches. He weighed two hundred and twenty pounds and not one bit of it was fat. His size, handsome features, and grace of movement made him to stand out among his people. He had long arms and wide shoulders. His black hair and dark complexion he got from his mother. He figured his height and curl in his hair came from the Scottish blood of his father. That fact alone was the single thorn wedged into his body and precisely why he was on his way west. The white blood was something he could not deny, but he did not have to like it. He was Cherokee.

He owed Red Wolf for his warrior and hunting skills. He also schooled him in the old ways of the Cherokee people. Because of Red Wolf, the forest was his home. It's smell always flooded his nose with the peaceful aroma of home. The beautiful quiet of a woodland without the sound of humans was a most enchanting thing to his ears. The sights of a bird in flight from one tree to another or a young deer peacefully drinking from a stream always calmed his spirit. Red Wolf had given birth to this part of his life as well as the skills of the great Cherokee heritage. There was no wasted motion in anything Rivers did. The building of a fire, working with a horse, or stalking a deer was done with such smoothness of action that a bystander would never recognize the burden of his work.

Rivers found his greatest obstacle in life to be the mixed blood of his family. Franklin Adair, a man of royal Scottish blood, had married his mother some twenty years ago. When Rivers asked her why she married a white man, she told him it was a common and accepted thing among her people. Rivers could not understand it. The Moravian missionaries had given his mother a Christian name. They called her Mary. Rivers never used it. He always called her No-qui-si, or Star, her Cherokee name. Rivers hated what the white people had done to his mother and his people. They had been robbed of their heritage.

Franklin Adair was such a man. He never liked the Cherokee in Rivers. Rivers did not help the situation. He made it quite obvious he did not like the white blood flowing through his body. He refused to speak the white man's language, though he knew it well and could converse with whites so well they would never suspicion him being an Indian. He refused the white man's religion. It was destructive to his people. They no longer fought to defend what was theirs. As a youngster, Rivers was a rebel in his family. The white man who was his father never gave him honor, love, respect, or made him feel wanted. His actions fueled Rivers resistence to anything that smelled of white man's ways.

Because of his dislike for his father, Rivers left home and lived with Red Wolf and his grandmother Raven when he was eleven years old. It hurt his mother for him to go, but she seemed to understand. She trusted Red Wolf and Raven to teach him well. His grandparents never accepted the white man's ways and Rivers was at home with them. In reality, they became his family. He and Red Wolf would go into the forest each day and Raven would cook what they brought home. Rivers learned the qualities of all the plants and tendencies of all the animals from Red Wolf.

At that moment, Rivers was startled out of his thoughts by some sound in the brush along the river and he quietly slipped away from the fire and eased toward the sound. He searched the area between him and the river. Finding nothing, he reasoned it was some animal and went back to the fire. The knife he held comfortably in his hand during the search took him back to his memories as he placed it by his blanket and threw a couple of small branches onto his fire.

The knife had been a gift of Red Wolf. It was his primary weapon. It had been made by a knife maker in Gainesville, Georgia. The blade and frame were forged from blended metals to keep a good edge. The blade was twelve inches long and two and a half inches wide at the guard. The point of the blade tapered upwards a bit and the first three inches of the top were honed and sharpened like the bottom. This helped when gutting animals. The handles were made of antler smoothed to fit his hand. The end of the handle had a sizeable rounded knob, ground down and smoothed to give it perfect balance.

Red Wolf taught Rivers to throw the knife with skilled precision. He learned to pull and throw it as a deadly blade or as a blunt force weapon with the knob on the handle hitting the target. He often killed small game with the blunt force. The knife became so natural in his hand he felt comfortable defending himself with it in the face of any enemy.

He was also skilled with the bow and had bought an old long rifle two years back. The rifle allowed him to take game at greater distances. He practiced until he could fire it and reload quickly. It was hard for him to take a white man's rifle and use it, but it might not be so bad if he used it to kill white men.

He allowed his thoughts to leave the teaching sessions with his knife and Red Wolf. He focused for a moment on his last day at his mountain home in Georgia. He remembered standing there enjoying the forest. He had stolen the beauty of that moment and enjoyed it like someone discovering love for the first time. He allowed the moisture of his world to soak in every crevice of his being. His world was changing. The Cherokee people were growing weaker. The white man was telling more lies and the Cherokee people agreed to more concessions. It was never enough. Their land would be next. The militia and government soldiers were already moving through his people disarming them. Talk was spreading that soon his people would be forcibly moved to some far away place. Rivers had never conceded anything to the white man. He never would. Before riding away from his home, he bathed in the smells and sights of his place and enjoyed the day. He knew he would never be back.

He remembered the day as if it had just happened. Suddenly the wind picked up. The large trees began to swing back and forth to it's music. A splattering of leaves rushed to the ground, pushed on by the wind. The big black stallion raised his head into the wind and tested it. Certain of no enemies, he lowered his head to the bucket of grain.

The instant the horse had raised his nose into the air, Rivers had given his attention to the scents and movement of the forest. The wind and sounds of rustling leaves masked the usual sounds around him. He was always a careful man, but now more so than ever before. Rivers was determined he would never be disarmed or forcibly moved to a place he did not choose. He would never be at the mercy of a white man. His goods were packed and ready to travel. He had been mapping out his plans since his last visit with his mother. He went over to brush his horse and relived the visit.

A friend had brought word to him that his mother wanted him to come. Rivers loved her and it had been hard to stay away from her and his sister Shining Waters. His sister's white name was Mary Lou. There were two brothers as well. Frank and Alfred were white and were the pride of his father. Mary Lou was so much like his mother you could not help but love her. She too loved the old ways of the Cherokee and cherished the times when she could talk to Rivers.

Rivers rode with haste to his mother's house on that day. The messenger said his mother was very sick. When he rode up to the house he was relieved to see no sign of Franklin Adair or the two boys. He was saddened Mary Lou was nowhere to be seen. He walked into the house and went to his mother's room.

He knelt beside her bed and looked at his sleeping mother. She had lost a lot of weight and her face looked weak and drawn.

"No-qui-si," he spoke softly.

She opened her eyes and smiled. "Rivers, I'm so glad you came."

"I did not know you were so sick Mother. I would have come sooner," Rivers said.

"It's all right. I have something very important to tell you and I was afraid I wouldn't get to. I feel like the sickness will soon win this battle," she said in a weak voice.

"No Mother. You are sick and need to rest. We can talk later."

"I must tell you, Rivers. I knew that I would some day. It is hard for me to do. I do not want to hurt you. You are such a fine man and I am so very proud of you."

"What do you mean? You cannot hurt me mother."

"I will not live long. I feel death already. Do not misunderstand. I am not afraid. The reason I must tell you is I am the only person who knows and it concerns you."

"Then tell me if you must. Do not worry. It will not hurt me."

Star paused for a minute and gathered her thoughts. Then she said,

"Listen. Do not stop me until I am finished. When I was a young woman, I fell in love with a white man. His name was Matthew McCloud. His family moved to our land after the big war between the Americans and the British. The Ross, Adair, and McCloud families all moved here at the same time. Matthew was a handsome man. He was three years older than me. His father and my father became friends and our families were close. There was a strong feeling between us from the first time we met. We talked of marriage. Then suddenly his family moved west. His father had arranged to buy some land somewhere and they left. It was not until they were gone that I realized I was going to have a baby. He did not know it. He would have never left me had he known. He promised me he would come back for me.

"I was so embarrassed. Franklin Adair had been trying to court me for a long time. I did not love him. To save face, I married Franklin. He never knew I was already with child. When you were born, he thought you were his. After your brothers were born, I believe he had doubts about being your father. You look so different from the other boys. He never mentioned it. I just felt it."

"You mean Franklin Adair is not my father?" Rivers shocked voice asked.

"I'm so sorry Rivers. I knew it would hurt you. I should have died with the secret."

"Oh no, Mother. It does not hurt. It is a relief. I have never liked the man. He has never treated me with respect. Oh, he would never do it so you would know, but he always made me feel unwanted. It is why I left," Rivers spurted out in an uncommon string of words.

"You are not ashamed of me?"

"No. I only wish you could have spent your life with the man you loved, even if he was a white man. Did he not ever come back for you?"

"No. I am not sure why. He could have been killed or something. The life there is much different from here I understand. I do know he loved me. You would have loved him too."

"No. If he broke his promise to return, then he is no different than all the white men. Promises mean nothing to them."

"Rivers, he was not that kind of man. Something happened to keep him away. I have thought of him every day since he left. After a while I hoped he would not return. I carried so much shame because I was going to have you and I was not married. I married only to save me and you the embarrassment. Afterwards I hoped he would not return and find me married. I will always believe he would have taken me with him had he known about you."

"Tell me about my father," Rivers said.

Star's voice was getting weaker as she said, "He was a good man. He worked hard. I've wanted to tell you so many times how he loved horses. They were his life."

Rivers thought, so it was not just the Indian in me that brought the love for horses.

Star continued, "He was a big man and so handsome. Yet, he was gentle, quiet, and very tender. The men talked about how no man would fight him for fear of being soundly whipped. He was a young girl's dream."

"Do you know where his family went when they moved west?"

"No. He just said they were moving west. A lot of people were going that way during those days."

"Thank you for telling me, Mother. I promise you I will find him some day."

"That would please me. If you do, tell him I died loving him." Tears spilled from her eyes and Rivers gently wiped them with his fingers.

"When you find him, will you give him this?" Star asked as she pulled a small leather bag from beside her bed. She opened it and took out a small broach. "He gave me this. Franklin never knew where it came from. Tell Matthew I cherished it to my death."

"I will Mother."

"Rivers, there is something else to tell you. The white people will come soon to take us away. I may not live until they do. I want you to leave now. Do not stay and let them take you. You can make it in the white man's world. I know you can. Do not stay because of me and Mary Lou. Franklin will care for her. I want you to be free. Please promise me you will leave and not come back." The tears were flowing freely now and Rivers dropped his head on her breast. "Promise me Rivers."

"Rivers lay there for a minute and then raised his head to look into her eyes. "I love you Mother. I promise you I will always be free." He placed his hand on her face and felt her warmth. Then he stood, looked down and smiled before he turned and walked away.

4

Rivers finally drifted off to sleep. So much had happened over the past few months and he could not erase the horrible events from his mind. As tired as he was, sleep was short and he came awake with fresh memories of his last days in his homeland.

The day he left his mother's house after his last visit with her, he traveled with a sad heart back to his home. He rode up to the cabin with a lot on his mind. A once proud people would soon be uprooted from their homeland. They would be forced to live where their life blood would slowly be drained away. It did not matter that the white man made the Indian territory sound like a wonderful place. It was all a lie. The white man never did anything to help the Indian. Rivers thought, I am happy my grandfather and grandmother are not here to go through this hurt. His grandfather would not have gone. He would have fled to the high mountains and fought to the death

His mother's illness was the other sad reality. A good and strong woman had been weakened by the fever. He could hear death in her breathing. It made Rivers proud that she was not afraid to die. He hoped he could face death with the same courage. Star was the guiding force in his life. To lose her would be to lose a part of himself. He had known it would happen someday. He wished to have her longer.

Rivers dismounted by his cabin and stripped the gear from his horse. He released him so he could go to the creek some fifty paces from his cabin and drink. The big horse drank his fill and then moved to graze on the green grass growing along the creek banks. It was a ritual he followed every time he came home.

Rivers walked over and flopped down on the small porch. He thought back over his visit with his mother. Learning Franklin Adair was not his father was both a surprise and a relief. He would have no trouble forgetting him. Matthew McCloud was a different matter. He confessed to himself that the first emotion he felt when his mother told him was to find McCloud and get to know him. It was followed quickly by the strong reminder of white men's lies. He wanted to dislike McCloud. Yet his mother gave McCloud a high and respected place in her heart. That alone was enough for Rivers to search for him. He would decide for himself about respecting him.

Rivers pushed these thoughts from his mind and breathed in the mountain air. He lay back and closed his eyes. The bubbling sound of the stream was a sleep medicine. He dozed off wishing life could be as simple and pure as the moment. Why couldn't life be a cool breeze, good water, fine horses, shelter, a warm bed, meat hanging, and no enemies in sight.

He awoke to the truth. Life was not simple. He had to get ready to travel. His future was west. Getting out of the mountains was his first priority. He whistled for his horse and put him in the small corral behind his cabin. He then went inside and started packing what he would take with him. Most of what he owned he would leave behind.

He used a wooden pack frame holding two large canvas bags to begin storing his travel goods. He walked to the back corner of his cabin and lifted two boards from the floor. Beneath the floor were eight bags that represented his future. They contained gold.

Red Wolf was the one who showed him one of the gold nuggets found in the stream running through his mountain hollow. The hollow itself was over a mile in length. The stream was sided by two steep mountains running back toward the high mountains. Red Wolf had brought him to this place when he was only ten years old. It was a special place for them and it was here Rivers chose to build his cabin and live after his grandparents died.

"See this shining stone," Red Wolf had said. "It is what the white man calls gold. It is worth a lot of the white man's money. Never speak of it. If you do, they will come and take it. They would kill you for it."

Rivers took Red Wolf's advice. It was his secret. It was after Red Wolf's death and about the time the white man started taking away the Cherokee's freedom of ownership of land that Rivers turned his mind to the gold. Until then he had no use for it.

He had found several good nuggets near a gully that brought rain water off the mountain. He followed it carefully and found more gold in the dry waterbed of the gully. About halfway up he found where a part of a rock wall had broken off as a result of frozen water during the winter. Shining bright in the remaining wall was a slab of gold. It was about six inches wide and ran a length of about five feet. Later Rivers came back and dug the soft gold out of the rocks. The eight bags were hidden for tomorrow. It was now tomorrow.

Rivers took the bags and split them between the two canvas bags of his pack. On top of them he placed his clothes, bedding, cooking gear, spare powder and shot, and cured meat. Satisfied he had everything he needed to travel, he tied the canvas bags tight and set the pack against the wall.

5

Rivers was not the kind of man to be melancholy or spend a lot of time living in the past. He never intended to let this night be one of remembering. The sight of the Cherokee people on the boats had been the key that opened his mind. What followed was a continuous flow of thoughts detailing his last days in Georgia. The memories kept on coming. He looked over to his black stallion and he was off to the past again.

He remembered walking outside to sit on his porch after he was packed and ready to travel. He knew the route he would take. As he mapped out his plans in his mind, two things surfaced as priorities. Before he left, he would visit his mother and sister one last time. He would then ride to the Griggs plantation. Amos Griggs had been a friend of his grandfather. Red Wolf told him to go to him if he ever needed help. Red Wolf told him Amos Griggs was a white man you could trust and keep the hair on your tail. Griggs was known for the horses he raised. Rivers worked for him breaking and training horses after his grandfather's death. A Griggs horse was a coveted animal in Georgia. In fact, the big black stallion Rivers rode was a Griggs horse.

Griggs had bought a stallion form France. The bloodline was of the old Anglo-Norman war horses. Bred for it's sturdy frame, the Anglo-Norman horse was indeed a war horse. Griggs bred the animal to American quarter horse mares he bought out of the early American Colonies. They were a mix of Spanish and English bloodlines.

One of the quarter horse mares on the Griggs plantation bore the stallion Rivers prided himself in as the best stallion in the country. It was born a sickly foal and never impressed Griggs at all. Rivers cared for it daily and upon learning Griggs was going to shoot it, he begged the plantation owner for it.

"Get it off my place and you can have it," Rivers recalled Griggs saying.

Rivers took the young foal to his place and after weeks on cow's milk laced with honey and herbs, the young colt began to grow and slick down.

Later, when Rivers rode the stallion onto the Griggs plantation for the first time, everybody marveled at the beautiful animal. Griggs wanted to buy it.

"Best looking stallion I've ever seen," Griggs had said.

Rivers turned him down. He named the horse War because of his Norman War Horse bloodline. He was now the most prized possession he had.

Rivers needed to see Griggs for another reason. Griggs was knowledgeable about money. Rivers knew he held in his possession enough raw gold to amount to a lot of money. He needed the white man's help in getting the gold into spendable money. He did not want to travel west with that much gold and not have anyone he could trust to help him. Red Wolf and his possum story continued to guide his life. With the money matter settled, he would then head west. Where he would go and where he would stop, he did not know.

Rivers rode away from his hidden hollow leading his packhorse laden with gold and his gear. His route to his mother's house was a seldom used trail coming down off the mountain behind their place. He often used it as a young boy and it would avoid the roads and perhaps the soldiers.

As he neared the house, he tied his horses and went on afoot. He carried his rifle just in case. He stopped a good hundred steps above the house and listened. It was strangely quiet. He could see the house clearly and part of the yard. There was no movement and no smoke from the chimney.

He slipped on through the trees and ran the last short distance to stand against the back wall. Something was wrong. Too quiet. He eased the back door open and his heart dropped. The house had been ransacked. The floor held the scattered remnants of his mother's belongings. He walked through the house, anger building within him. The furniture was gone. Everything useful had been taken. He walked to the front door and looked down toward the barn and meadow beyond it. The livestock were gone. Weighted down wagon ruts in the front yard told the story. The family had been taken and others came to strip the house.

Rivers rushed back through the house and up the hill to his horses. Forgetting the back trails for the moment, he rode down by the house and hit the road following the ruts of the wagons. It was in Rivers favor he didn't look like an Indian. His curly hair was cut to barely curl over his ears and neck. He was wearing a western hat, a bleached blue shirt, and cotton pants. His buckskin pants and shirts were packed away. His boots were white man's boots. He was even using a western saddle. He preferred no saddle at all. Yet, he knew he had to look the part if he was to make it west in the white man's world.

He followed the wagon tracks. They had looked fresh at his mother's house and were looking fresher now. He rounded a curve and saw them up ahead. It was only one wagon. The others must have rode off ahead with lighter loads. As he rode near he counted the heads of two men.

Rivers came up to them and cantered on by, raising his hand in a wave. When he was in front of them far enough, he pulled up and blocked the road. His rifle lay across his saddle. He had never seen the men before. He knew the contents of their wagon well. It was his mother's things. The men looked like a rough sort.

"You fellows moving?" Rivers asked.

"Naw," the driver answered as he squirted a string of tobacco juice into the dirt, leaving some on his chin. He wiped it off with the back of his hand. "I don't know whur you headed, but you shure missin out. The sodgers are roundin up the injuns and movin them out. Their belongins are free for the takin."

"You mean you can just go take their things after they are gone?" Rivers asked.

"Yesiree. We follered along behind the sodgers. After they drug the redskins off, we just loaded up."

"Did you see the Indians these things belonged to?" Rivers asked.

"Yep. A squaw man, his woman, and three growed kids. One of em a purty girl. Wish they'd let me have her," the driver said with a belly laugh. The other man laughed with him.

"It's a shame you have gone to all this work for nothing," Rivers said.

"What you mean for nothing? This stuff will bring some dollars in Gainesville."

"What I mean is you won't be selling it," Rivers replied.

It took a minute for the stranger's words to register with the rabble. When it did, they started for their guns. Rivers was faster and swung his rifle, leveling it on the driver. They both sat staring at him with evil eyes.

"What you up to man?" the other man asked. "You planning on robbing us?"

"No. I'm not a thief. Right now I'm fighting the urge to kill you. Whether I do or not depends on you. I really don't care," Rivers said in a low, emotionless voice. "Get down slow. Leave your rifles in the wagon."

The two men did not like it, but they did what he said.

"Start walking. Don't look back. If you do, I'll shoot," Rivers said.

They left out at a fast pace a little short of a run. Neither risked a glance back. Rivers swung down and unhooked the mules from their harness. He threw the harness in the wagon and walked the mules behind it. With a slap and yell he sent them running back the way they had come. He then looked at the contents of the wagon. It was a sad moment. He fished out a match and started his mother's bedding on fire. He piled some other cloth material on it and in a matter of minutes the entire wagon was blazing.

He mounted up and rode a short distance away to escape the heat. He sat watching his mother's belongings burn. No white dirt will sleep on her bed, he thought. He pulled around and headed for Gainesville. He now rode away from the road. He knew it would be days before he dared to take to the roads again. After about an hour, some of his anger started to subside.

6

Rivers rode onto the Griggs plantation late the same afternoon. He headed for the house and tied his horses out under a tree. He saw one of the house servants and asked him to tell Mr. Griggs he wanted to speak with him. A few minutes later the tall slender owner of the plantation walked out to where he was.

"Come on up to the porch and have a seat," Amos Griggs said. Griggs looked over at the loaded horses and spoke as they were walking to the house. "Are you headed somewhere?"

They took a seat in some porch chairs as Rivers replied, "I'm heading west. I need to get my pay and I want to talk to you about a couple of things before I go."

"What's your hurry," Griggs asked.

"You know the government is rounding up my people and moving them to the place they call the Indian Territory. I'm Cherokee, and I'm not going."

"Didn't think you would. If your grandfather was alive, he wouldn't be going either," Griggs said with a smile. "I can help you if you want to stay here. I promise you they won't touch you."

"I believe you Mr. Griggs. You are the only white man I respect. I enjoy working for you. But my future is in the west. I plan on buying me some land out there somewhere and raise horses like you. That is one of the things I need to talk to you about."

"That'll take money boy. You've got about two hundred dollars coming from me, but that won't buy much land." Rivers had asked Griggs earlier to hold his pay until he asked for it.

"I'll tell you how I plan to do that later. The first thing I want to do is make you an offer."

Griggs smiled at Rivers, amused that this young man was making him an offer. "What's your offer?"

"I know you have always wanted my horse ever since you saw him full grown."

"You bet I do. He's the best stallion in the country as far as I'm concerned. I'd pay you top dollar for him," Griggs quickly replied.

Rivers smiled and said, "He's still not for sale. My offer is to stay here for about three weeks and let you breed him to as many of your mares you can during that time."

Griggs attention raised. "You mean you are offering me his services. What do you want in return?"

"When I get settled out west, I'll send word where I am. Your pay for my horse's services will be ten of your best three year old mares that are not of my horse's bloodline. You would have to pay whoever brings them to me."

Griggs laughed out loud. "Boy, you've been doing some thinking, haven't you? You walk up here offering me the stud service of the best horseflesh I've ever seen and you know I can't turn that down. To be honest, I'd pay a lot more."

"I don't want more. If it was not for you, I wouldn't own War. I believe ten of your mares matched with him would put me on the map out west."

"Rivers, I'm proud of you. I've always known you would amount to something. I'll accept your offer and I'll help you any way I can."

Rivers thanked him and said, "I appreciate it. I need your help on another matter right now."

"How can I help?"

"If I had a good sum of money and wanted to travel without the risk of it being stolen, how would you suggest I do it?"

"I'll tell you how I do it. I put my money in the bank and get a letter from the bank telling how much money I have to spend. Banks have ways of dealing with each other through these letters without you having to carry cash money around."

"Do you trust the bank?"

"I trust mine. I own it," Griggs said with a smile.

"You own a bank?" Rivers asked in astonishment.

"Yes. I hire people to run it for me. It is The People's Bank in Gainesville."

"Would you help me get such a letter?"

"I sure would. How much money you got?" Griggs asked while thinking, surely he does not have much.

"I really don't know. I need you to help me on that too."

"What do you mean you don't know?"

Rivers leaned closer and said in a low voice, "It is gold I'm carrying."

"Gold," Griggs said in surprise. "You've got gold. How much?"

"I've got eight pretty big sacks of it. Is there a way I can trade it for money?"

Griggs laughed again. "There sure is. Where do you have your gold stored?"

"On my pack horse."

"I can't believe this. You are riding around with eight sacks of gold. Man, there are plenty of people around here who would kill you for one nugget. If we hurry, we can get to town before the assayer's office closes. Let me get a horse."

Griggs yelled for a horse to be brought around and in a few minutes they were riding for town.

At the assayer's office Griggs went inside while Rivers fished one sack out of his pack. He took it inside and Griggs had the man who ran the office close and lock the door. The man's name was Phillips. Rivers handed Phillips the heavy sack and he spilled it's contents out on a table.

"My God," Phillips said. "Where did you get this?"

"That's not important and it is none of your business," Griggs answered. We want you to put a value on it. What's it worth?" Griggs asked. His eyes were big too, taking in the gold ore.

Phillips studied it, tested it with some instruments and liquids, and then sacked it back up and put it on a scale. He did a little figuring and then said, "Mr. Griggs, I'd say the contents of this sack is worth at least ten thousand dollars. It's some of the finest ore I've ever seen."

Rivers drew in a deep breath. "Would you say that again?"

"I said ten thousand dollars."

Griggs thanked Phillips for his time and paid him five dollars for his labor. Griggs and Rivers then walked outside.

"You say you have eight of those bags?"

"Yes."

"Are they all the same size?"

"Just about. Some may be a little heavier than the others. I didn't worry much about that."

"Tell you what let's do. We'll take the gold and put it in the safe at my bank. I'll arrange for you to have a letter of credit saying you have eighty thousand dollars on deposit in my bank. That letter will allow you to conduct any business you want to with your money. It will mean that when you buy your land, you will have to arrange for somebody to come and get the money. But you can conduct your business on the promise of it coming. Most folks would deal with you on that basis. I'll also give you any cash you need for traveling out of the gold. Phillips is known to estimate the value of gold low. When we find out it's true worth, I'll make sure anything over eighty thousand dollars goes into your account."

"Then let's do it."

"Let's get to the bank and get the gold in there for safe keeping."

"Mr. Griggs, you didn't ask me where I got the gold."

"It ain't none of my business. Come on."

Rivers stopped him. "That's why I respect you."

Griggs smiled and motioned for him to follow. When the gold was in the safe at the bank, they headed back toward the plantation.

Griggs spoke as they rode, "Well, now I see how you planned on buying some land out west. You need to understand you are a wealthy man by today's standards. You must handle it with care. There are a lot of people out there who will trick you out of it if you let them."

"It's been a long time since I've been tricked," Rivers said. "I want to thank you for helping me. Red Wolf always told me to come to you if I needed help. He trusted you."

"You're welcome Rivers. I thought a lot of your grandfather. Did I ever tell you how we met?"

"No."

"You know how he loved horses. He wanted a Griggs horse and showed up here one day ready to talk trade." Griggs smiled as he remembered it. "He offered me three pretty fair mares for one of mine. Now, my mares sold for a lot more than the three horses he brought with him would have sold for. I told him I couldn't make the trade. Well, he looked me straight in the eye and asked if I had any horses I was having trouble breaking. To be honest I had about ten at the time, but I didn't know why he was asking that. He offered to break them for me free of charge if I would trade with him. I took him up on it and he handled my horses like they were babies. He had them eating out of his hand in no time. I couldn't believe how he could break a horse without all the problems most folk have. When he was finished, I gave him his Griggs mare and just took one of his. We became friends on the spot and remained so until his death."

"So, grandfather worked his magic on you?"

"Yes, he did. And I was almighty proud. He broke horses for me after that. He didn't work here all the time. I would get word to him when I had a difficult bunch and he would show up and take care of them."

"He was a great man," Rivers said.

"He sure was. Now let's get home. I want to get all the use out of your stud horse I can before you leave. You gave me three weeks didn't you?"

"Yes. If you don't mind, I'll stay with you until I leave. It might be a little dangerous for me anywhere else."

"You have a place to eat and sleep for as long as you like. I noticed the old long rifle you are carrying. There's a lot of fur trappers going west.

It's a big business. I hear they are all carrying what they call a plains rifle. It uses a percussion cap and it's a lot easier to reload and shoot. It don't have all the frills of the Kentucky rifle. Mostly stock and barrel. The barrel is made of a softer metal and it shoots a lot straighter. Some folks in Tennessee have copied the people in Missouri and are making a plains rifle with a shorter barrel. It handles real well. I bought me one. Hawkes Gunsmith store in Gainesville has some. I'd suggest you trade for one and get yourself a couple of percussion cap pistols. Things are different in the west Rivers. There ain't no law. There are plenty of rough white men you will need to steer clear of. From what I hear there are also a lot of Indians who wouldn't care if you are Cherokee. You better get yourself the right weapons and plenty of caps, powder, and shot to last you a while. You can use the time while your are here to get used to loading and shooting. Believe me, it will come in handy. You just tell Justin Hawkes I told you to get what you want and put it on my account. We'll settle up later."

"I appreciate that Mr. Griggs. I've been wondering what I would need in the way of weapons. I've got my bow and knife, but I guess I do need something to take care of my enemies from a greater distance."

"You sure do.

The three weeks passed quickly. I got the rifle and pistols like Mr. Griggs suggested and was amazed at how quickly I learned to shoot and reload. I was good with them and became more comfortable each day. I spent the rest of my time thinking about my mother and sister. I decided that I would go take them away from the Indian Territory. I couldn't bear to think about them being forced to live there.

The day arrived for me to leave the plantation. I took the last conversation I had with Mr. Griggs as an opportunity to learn about raising horses.

"In the west, I am told, the two important factors you must consider when buying land to raise livestock are water and grass. I would think you would also need to think about wintering them if you get far enough north to have to deal with snow," Griggs told him.

"I plan on starting with a brood mare herd of about twenty. I'll build it a little each year. Raising horses will be easy for me. It's the business side I'll really have to learn."

"That will come easy enough. Ask high. You will be raising horses a cut above everything around you because of your stallion. When people buy your horses and pay more, your reputation spreads quickly. If they don't want to pay your price, just tell them to settle for an average horse somewhere else. I promise you that stallion will sire no average horses."

"Mr. Griggs, do you remember the McCloud family that used to live around here? I would imagine they left here about twenty years ago."

Griggs was a little taken by the shift in the conversation. "Sure I remember the McClouds. I bought a couple of mares from Oscar McCloud. He had some good horses. Why do you ask about them?"

"Oh, I just heard from some of my people he was good with horses and left here to go out west to start a horse operation. Do you happen to remember where he went when he left?"

"No. But it's strange you mention McCloud. I was talking to a man about six months ago who was raving about a McCloud horse he bought off a man who had returned here from Texas. He told me owning a McCloud horse out west was like owning a Griggs horse in Georgia. I saw the horse. It was a beautiful animal. Tried to buy it but the man wouldn't sell."

Rivers handled the word Texas like it had flown right by him. It hadn't. He said, "That's interesting. I hope the time comes when owning a Rivers horse will mean something."

Griggs paid Rivers the money he owed him, handed him a leather bag holding twenty thousand dollars in gold coins minted in Gainesville, and wished him well.

"I'll be waiting to hear where you want your mares delivered," Griggs said.

"I'll get word to you. Thank you for everything," Rivers said.

The two men shook hands and Rivers headed out atop his big stallion and trailing his packhorse. He had a ways to go and a lot to do. It felt good to him to be on his way.

Dawn was breaking when Rivers realized he had spent the entire night reliving his recent days. Coming out of the memories was a resolve to find his mother and sister. He also knew one day he would find Matthew McCloud. Pushing the memories aside, he fried some cured meat over the fire and ate before loading his packhorse and moving out.

7

Rivers followed the Tennessee river from a distance. He was less likely to run into anybody by staying away from the river. Houses and farm land was becoming more of a presence. He rode up to one farm house with the intent of buying some food. It had been a while since he had eaten an egg. The farmer was more than willing to sell him some eggs and bacon.

"I'm going to the far west," Rivers told him. "What track would be the best for me to take?"

"If'n I was you, I'd stay with the Tennessee until it turns north. It runs mostly due west all the way across the rest of Alabama. When she takes the northern turn, I'd keep going straight west until I hit the Mississippi river You'll have to take a ferry across the Mississippi. Too wide and deep to swim. Or if you're a mind to, you could get on one of them boats over at Waterloo and ride to St. Louis. There's a lot of boat traffic now a days with them hauling all them Indians."

"Are they bringing Indians through here?"

"Yep. They haul them to Decatur and stop there. Decatur's just about a day's ride from here. The reason they stop there is the river is too shaller for boats all the way to Waterloo. They take them Indians off and send them on a steam train to Tuscumbia. Then they make them walk to Waterloo where they get on another boat. Least that's what the soldiers told me the other day.

"Have you seen any of the Indians?"

"Sure have. Me and the wife and younguns went to Decatur the last week. We set down and watched them unload them Indians. It was a pitiful sight. A lot of them was sick. Ain't no way to treat nobody. I don't care if they are Indians."

"I feel the same way. Thanks for your help and I appreciate you selling me the eggs and bacon."

"You're plumb welcome. Be careful on your travel. I hear them Indians can be fearsome mean out where you're headed."

Rivers smiled at the thought of him being careful of Indians and waved goodbye as he rode out of the yard. He had his mother and sister on his mind as he rode toward Decatur. He would go to where the boats tie up and see what he could learn.

He found the town of Decatur perched on the southern bank of the river. He rode down to the river's edge and made his way to the docks. A number of flatboats and one steamboat were tied up there. They were the same boats he saw filled with Indians yesterday. He saw a group of workers and soldiers sitting off to one side. He dismounted and sidled over near them, keeping his eyes on the boats. He saw no sign of life on them. One of the workers came walking by and Rivers stopped him.

"What they doing with all the flatboats?" he asked the man.

"Transporting Indians," he replied. "Brought in a big load of them yesterday. Put them on a train headed for Tuscumbia as soon as they got here."

"Where were the Indians from?" Rivers questioned.

"Cherokees from North Carolina and Georgia. In bad shape too. They unloaded seven who died on the way here. Mostly old folks. The soldiers always stop here and go back with the boats for another load. Wouldn't surprise me if them Indians don't escape between here and Tuscumbia."

"I wonder why the soldiers stop here."

"They say it's their orders. Say them Indians ain't got nowhere to go except where they are headed. They always put one of them in charge of the train ride and tell him who to talk to when they get to Tuscumbia."

"How far is it to Tuscumbia?"

"It's about a day and a half ride. Them Indians will stay over in Tuscumbia for a couple of days to rest up. Then they'll walk to where the river gets deep again and load up on a boat."

"Well, you have a good day," Rivers said as he led his horses on down the river front. A little later he mounted up and headed toward Tuscumbia. He rode until dark before making camp. He was back on the trail early and came into Tuscumbia late in the afternoon.

Tuscumbia sat back from the high bluffs that guarded the southern shore of the river. He found the area around the town covered with Indians. Most of them were camped by a big spring just south of town. He rode through their camp with his eyes open for a face he could recognize. He saw nobody familiar. He came up the hill from the spring and tied his horses at the livery. He arranged for them to be fed. He saw Indians walking in and out of shops and stores all over the town.

He left his horses and walked to main street looking for anybody from his homeland. He heard the Cherokee language clearly as the Indians talked among themselves. He saw two Cherokee men standing off to one side.

"Where was your homeland?" Rivers asked in the Cherokee tongue.

"We are from the high mountains of North Carolina," one answered. "You speak our language. Are you Cherokee?"

"Yes. I'm looking for my mother and sister. They were taken from Georgia."

"They left in the first groups. There are enough in the stockades back there for many more trips," the other man said.

"Do the soldiers not guard you here?"

"No. Many who live in Tuscumbia are of Indian blood. They have given us clothes, blankets, and food. It is good to find people with a heart. They told the authorities there was no need to guard us in their town."

"Why do you not run away?"

"We have no place to go. We have no food for travel. We would die or be killed," the first Indian said.

"Have many died on your journey?"

"Yes. Out of our boats there have been eleven to die. The soldiers threw some of their bodies into the water. It was hard for us to watch."

In the middle of their conversation Rivers saw a familiar face across the street. It was Deer Foot, one of his people. Rivers dashed across the street.

"Deer Foot," he called out.

The Indian turned at the sound of his name and was surprised to see Rivers. The two men clasped each other's arms in a welcome gesture.

"Rivers, what are you doing here?"

"I came looking for my mother and sister. Have you seen them?"

"I was taken when they were. They were put on the boats first. My family is with them. I was left behind because the boats were full." Deer Foot lowered his eyes and with a sad voice said, "Rivers, your mother died before the boats left."

Even though he expected it, the news ripped Rivers to the heart. "Were you there?"

"Yes. We helped bury her on the high ground off from the river. Your father, brothers, and sister left the next day on the boats.

Rivers gathered himself for a minute. Then he stepped close to Deer Foot. "Do you know where they took my sister?"

"They told me to come to the Neosho Creek and follow it north. They said our people would be living along the creek."

"Do you want to leave with me? I will not live under the white man's guns. I would be honored if you would go with me," Rivers said.

"I would like to, but I can't. My family needs me. I must continue the journey."

"Would you find my sister when you get there. Tell her you saw me. Do not tell the others. Tell her to be strong. I will come for her as soon as I have a place for her to live. Will you do that for me?"

"You dream, Rivers. You will never have a place in the white man's world. However, I will tell her your words."

"Thank you. Take care of yourself and be strong." Rivers thought for a moment, then asked, "Did not any of our people fight?"

"Some tried, but it was hopeless," Deer Foot said. After a minute of reflection, he continued, "There was Tsali. Did you hear about him?"

"No. Tell me."

"The soldiers came and took him and his family. His wife could not walk fast so the soldiers pushed her with the long knives on their rifles. It angered Tsali so that he and his sons attacked the soldiers. One soldier was killed and the others ran. Tsali and his people escaped."

"Then I am proud of Tsali."

"The story is sad. The soldiers sent out messengers saying that the men responsible should surrender so their women and children would not be harmed. Tsali and his sons came in and the soldiers tied them up. They brought Cherokee men from the stockades and made them shoot the captives."

"It is not sad for Tsali and his sons. They fought. They were warriors. It was a sad day for the Cherokee men who were used by the white men. Tonight, when I sit by my fire, I will sing the death songs for Tsali and his sons. They make me proud."

The two clasped arms again and Rivers walked quietly away. He would ride out now. He couldn't wait to be alone, build a fire, and sing the death songs. He went for his horses and left the town by riding down the hill to the big spring. Before he left the livery he asked the man working there how far it was to the Mississippi river from Tuscumbia. The man responded that it was at least five hard days riding headed due west. Rivers stopped on his way out of town and took in the host of Cherokees camped at the spring. The area around the spring was covered with makeshift shelters for the hundreds of Cherokee gathered there. Fires were burning and pots of boiling stew sent a familiar aroma into the air. He looked at the people. They were a people of the wounded spirit. Rivers wondered how the white man could live with the shame of what he was seeing being done to his people. His heart heavy, Rivers rode away.

His camp for the night was some eight miles out of Tuscumbia. Settled on the back side of a ridge a short distance from the river, he sat by his fire and remembered the soft hands and warm breasts of the woman who truly loved him. He thought of her smile and beautiful eyes. He now knew why her love for him was so special. He was her child and that kind of love is natural. But there was more. I was the son of the man she truly loved.

He remembered the greatest advice she ever gave him. He could still hear her words. "Listen to Red Wolf. Learn from him. Your spirit will be strong and your word true if you learn from him. Even though he is old now, he is still proud. The old ways have been good for him. They will be good for you."

8

Rivers held his westerly course and came up on the Mississippi river on his sixth day out of Tuscumbia. He had ridden from early to late each day, stopping only to replenish his supplies once at a small farm. When he got close enough to see the river it caused him to gasp. He had never seen anything like it. It ran slow and wide. No wonder the man back in Alabama told him he would need to find a ferry.

He made camp along the bank of the river. He tied his horses back in the trees and built his fire well enough away from the river to attract no attention. He sat against a tree and watched the peaceful river up until it was nearly dark. There was traffic along the river, but it all was up against the western bank. He figured he would have to ride north or south to find a ferry. He would make up his mind about which way tomorrow. After some supper of beans and meat, he settled in for the night.

Morning brought a misty rain that you couldn't see, but could feel. His fire felt good and after breakfast he put it out, loaded his packhorse and got ready to move on. He was about to ride out when he heard a bump of wood against wood and looked out on the river to see a flatboat coming down his side, close to the bank. They had a man on each side with poles and looked like a man in the back guiding it.

Rivers walked to the river's edge and yelled out to the men on the boat. "Which way to the closest ferry?"

"It's a long way which-ever way you go," one of the men yelled back.

"It don't matter. I've got to cross," Rivers shouted back. "I can pay if you would help me."

The man on the boat doing the talking yelled back, "There's some eddy water bout a mile downstream. We can pull in above the sand bar and get to the bank. If your horses will load over the high sides of our boat, then we could take you a few miles downstream to a place where we can tie up on the other side. Cost you five dollars. You got that much?"

"I can pay and I appreciate it. I'll meet you there."

"Hop to it. We ain't got all day."

Rivers did a little more cleaning up around his camp and swung into the saddle to head downstream. They were tying the boat up to some trees when he got there. He tied his packhorse to a tree and walked War down to the bank and into the shallow water. War stepped onto the boat without any problem. He then brought the packhorse down and after a little coaxing he stepped aboard as well.

"That's some kind of horse you're riding mister. Wouldn't want to sell him would you?" the man in charge asked.

"Nope. I couldn't do without him. Here's your five dollars," Rivers said, handing the man his money. "Sure appreciate you helping me. I've never seen a river this wide."

"First time to see this old muddy thing, eh?"

They were already untied and pushing the boat back into the flow of the river.

"Where you headed?" the man asked.

"The Oklahoma territory. I've got a job there helping the government get the Indians settled. I'm from out of Georgia. Could you tell me how you would get there?" Rivers asked. He made up the part about having a job there so they wouldn't ask him any more questions about his destination.

"They are taking a lot of them by boat. They come down the Mississippi and hit the Arkansas river way south of here. The Arkansas runs all the way up into Oklahoma. The boats can go most of the way there. I hear they are unloading them somewhere around Fort Smith. It sits close to the river. If I was you I'd keep on west. You'll cross the White river and then the Arkansas will be the second big stream you come to. You can follow it and you'll wind up at Fort Smith. The Indian territory is just past there."

They drifted along for a while and then headed in to the west bank. It didn't take long for Rivers to get his horses off the boat. He waved to the men as the boat pushed away from the bank. He looked back across the river and chuckled to himself. He thought, I'd be walking right now if I had tried to swim them horses across that thing.

When he left the Mississippi he found more flat land for the best of four days. He crossed what he figured was the White River on the third day. Two days later he was in some hill country and came out of it after three days to find the Arkansas. He headed upstream and stayed close enough to the river to keep his direction and far enough away from it to travel easier and avoid people. The weather was getting cooler. He knew he had to get somewhere before winter hit. He had noticed a little frost on the ground a couple of mornings. His coat had felt good until about mid morning for the last week.

He was in heavily wooded hill country now with the landscape looking more and more like Georgia, except there were no high mountains. He saw people on numerous occasions, but he kept his distance. He chose his camps at night for safety and protection. He never assumed he was safe. He took precautions by placing himself where it would be hard for anybody to get to him without making a lot of noise. While riding he kept the two pistols in his saddle bags, but come night he laid them close.

Eight days after hooking up with the Arkansas, the river basin opened up and he rode for another day in the foothills of the mountains. He camped close to the river and a little before sundown he sat by it and watched the flow of the water heading back where he had come from. He thought, the water passing me right now will be at the spot where I came up to the river in a lot less time than it took me to get here. His admiration for the world around him was a constant comfort.

He broke camp the next morning to a light frost and found the settlement surrounding Fort Smith before it was time to take off his coat. He rode in and found a livery stable. He left his horses there for a good feeding. They had settled for grass over the past two weeks. With his saddle bags, containing his pistols and gold coins, draped over his shoulder and rifle in hand, Rivers walked to a business that offered food and a place to sleep. A sign next door advertised a place to get a bath. He went first and rented a room. Next came the bath. He put on clean colthes and left his dirty clothes to be washed. He then went to eat.

He ordered a big plate of roast beef and potatoes. He sat quietly to one side of the café. The crowd dwindled down to one other man who happened to be sitting close by.

"How far is it to where they are putting all the Indians they are moving out of the east?" Rivers asked the man.

"Depends on which ones," the man answered. "Got'em scattered all over the territory."

"I came from Alabama and I saw them moving a lot of Cherokees. What about them?"

"Most of them are going up northeast of here about seventy-five miles. They are putting them all the way to the Missouri line I hear. The talk is the place is covered up with them."

"What kind of land are they putting them on. Is it good for crops and hunting?" Rivers asked.

"Nah. Mostly land wouldn't anybody with good sense want. I'd sure hate to be them redskins trying to make it through the winter."

Rivers grunted a response and broke off the conversation. He had his sister on his mind. The thought of her spending a horrible winter without food or shelter was more than he could handle. He had to get a place to settle in before winter hit. Then he would map out his plans to go get her.

He woke early the next day, picked up his clean clothes after breakfast, and walked to the livery to get his horses.

"Do you know of any ranches around here where a man might get a job for the winter?" he asked the hostler.

"Ain't many ranches around here. Probably the only one who might need somebody is Orvil Peter's place. Goes by the name of Crooked Wind ranch. It's about a half day's ride due north. He sells beef to the government for the soldiers and he raises horses to resupply the army."

"Thanks. I may ride by that way and see if he could use me. Gonna get cold before long and I'd like to find a place before it does."

Rivers rode out and headed due north.

9

About mid-morning Rivers began to see cattle grazing. He rode close and noticed the brand. It looked like two snakes side by side. It had to be the Crooked Wind brand. He saw a number of groups of cattle before he topped out on a knoll and saw the ranch buildings in the distance. He rode down and passed through a gate. It bore the name Crooked Wind. When he rode up to the gathering of buildings two men walked out to meet him. They came from the direction of what he figured to be their sleeping quarters.

"Howdy," one of them said. "What can we do for you?"

"My name is Rivers. I'm looking for some work through the winter if you need anybody," Rivers replied. "Would also appreciate somebody to talk to. Been talking to myself for a while." Rivers smiled at the man as he said it.

"I'm Flannigan," the man said with a laugh. "This here is Bostick. I've been there before. I know what you mean by wanting to hear somebody else besides yourself talking. I can't help you with the job. Mr. Peters, he's the owner, and our foreman Dolf Freeman are down at Fort Smith. They'll be back tomorrow. Why don't you climb down and eat with us. You can sleep in our bunkhouse tonight and talk to them in the morning."

"I appreciate that. It sure sounds good to me," Rivers replied.

The men took him inside the bunkhouse and motioned to a bunk over in the corner.

"Take that one. Most of the men are out bringing the cattle in close getting ready for cold weather. We got plenty of hay stored up. We keep a little grazing through the cold months, but we have to carry them with hay. We've got sixteen hands working here. They will come in sometime after dark tonight. Me and Bostick are looking after the place while they are gone," Flannigan said.

Rivers threw his stuff on the bunk and they walked to the building where they ate. After a good meal the threesome talked the afternoon away. Rivers enjoyed his time with the white men and actually liked them. He wondered if they would have been so fast to treat him like a guest if they knew he was an Indian.

They talked into the night and fell asleep after the talking died down. He heard the other hands come in long after he had gone to sleep. This would be a good place to spend the winter, he thought. I hope they can use me.

Rivers rolled out with the others and went to eat before daylight. Flannigan introduced him to the other men. They nodded and went about their business of eating without any conversation. They looked a little worn out. After breakfast the place became a buzz of men going about different jobs. Some rode out to check the cattle they had brought in and others were busy getting some horses up to the holding pens by the corral. They were going to get started breaking them. At least that's what Flannigan said they were going to do. He looked the men over who seemed to have the assignment and he didn't see anybody who stood out as knowing much about horses.

Rivers found himself a sunny spot beside one of the buildings and sat down to warm. He leaned back and enjoyed the moment. He must have dozed off. He woke a couple of hours later to see two men riding into the ranch yard. One of the men rode on up to the main house and a big fellow who looked the part of boss rode over toward the corral where the men were working the horses. Rivers stood up, brushed himself off, and walked over his way.

"Are you the foreman?" Rivers asked. "If you are, I'd like to talk to you about a job."

"I'm Dolf Freeman," the strong built man who looked to be in his forties said. "What kind of job you looking for?"

Freeman swung down and Rivers walked over to shake his hand.

"My name is Rivers. I'm really just looking for work to get me through the winter. I'll do anything, but I guess I'm best at breaking horses."

While they were talking a commotion broke out inside the corral. A big burly man was obviously mad at a horse he was trying to break. The man had the horse tied to a pole in the middle of the corral. In a spill of cussing the man walked quickly to the fence and picked up a heavy stick. He walked back to the horse and swung the stick, hitting the horse on the side of it's head.

Without thinking or saying a word, Rivers rushed to the pole fence and in a swift movement put his hands on the top rail and bounced over. He ran to the man as he raised the stick for another blow. Rivers grabbed the man's wrist, bending it sharply and causing the man to drop the stick.

"What the hell," the man said as he backed up while rubbing his wrist. His eyes took in the tall stranger standing calmly in front of him. "What do you think you're doing?"

Rivers spoke in a voice so low the men around the corral had to strain to hear. "Hitting an animal while it is tied is the way of a coward. Are you a coward?"

The big man spewed out a string of cuss words and finally got down to talking. "You ain't carrying no gun and it's a good thing. I'd shoot you right where you stand."

Rivers noticed for the first time the man had a flintlock stuck in his belt. He turned away and walked a calculated eight steps before he turned to face him. "I'm not wearing a gun because I don't need one," Rivers said. "I'm going to give you the chance to shoot me and all I've got is my knife. Before you make up your mind, I want you to know you will regret trying to shoot me."

The man looked around at the ranch hands gathered along the fence. He looked a little confused. This stranger didn't look scared. "You heard him. He told me to shoot if I want to. I don't want it said I killed a man who wasn't packing a gun. Ya'll heard him didn't you?"

The man looked at the ranch hands, but nobody said a word. The only sound was the heavy breathing of the horse as it pulled against the rope.

"I don't know who you are feller, but you done messed with the wrong man. I ain't gonna kill you. I'm just gonna shoot you up a mite," the man said through tobacco stained teeth.

Rivers did not reply. He stood calmly with his long arms hanging by his side. His big knife rode his leg, touching his finger tips.

The man reached to pull his pistol out of his belt. In a blur hard to follow, Rivers pulled his knife and threw it, leaving himself in a crouched position in front of the man. The blunt end of the knife hit the big man in the center of his forehead and knocked him as cold as a wedge. The pistol fell harmlessly to the ground. Rivers walked over, retrieved his knife, and went back to where Dolf Freeman was standing.

Rivers spoke first to the men along the fence. "Tell him he's lucky to be alive when he comes around," Rivers said.

"Mister, you've bought yourself some grief. That man is Roscoe Durham. He's plumb mean. He'll be out for you when he does come around," one of the cowhands said.

"I won't be hard to find," Rivers replied. "Now Mr. Freeman, I was talking to you about a job before all that. Do you need anybody? I'll work hard."

"I've never seen anything like what you just did feller. That was fast. What if you had missed," Freeman asked.

"I don't hardly ever miss. What about the job?"

"What if you hadn't knocked him out? He could have shot you."

"I intended to knock him out. If I hadn't, the knife would have been about twenty-five inches lower and sticking twelve inches into his chest."

"You mean to tell me you can throw the knife either way?"

"What I'm telling you is I can choose to kill a man or let him live. Now, about the job?"

Freeman stood with a look of amazement all over him. "You say your name is Rivers. You got a first name?"

"Rivers is enough."

"Well, Rivers, you got yourself a job. We've got about thirty head of horses we got to break and get ready for army remounts. If you think you can handle it, put your gear in the bunkhouse."

"It's already there. Do I need to see Mr. Peters?"

"You've heard about the boss, eh. No, you don't have to see him. I do the hiring and firing. Speaking of which, I been puttin off firing Durham for a spell."

"Don't fire him on my account. If he can do the job you hired him for, keep him on. He won't be no trouble for me."

"You don't know him."

"No, I don't. But I've known people like him. Any man who'll hit a horse is a coward. I know it and he knows it. You do what you got to, but don't fire him because of me. I been roping my own horse all my life."

"I'll think it over. You be careful around him. Get settled in and you can go to work on them horses in the morning. Fair enough?"

"Fair enough. Thanks for the job."

"You didn't ask how much we pay."

"It's going to get cold soon. Whatever you pay and the warm bed and food will be fine with me." Rivers smiled as he walked toward the bunkhouse.

Rivers was removing some of his things from his pack when he noticed movement in the doorway. He turned to face a big lanky man who stood almost as tall as he did and probably weighed as much. The man walked over an stuck out his hand.

"The name's Sharp. Folks call me Goldy because of this hair I'm wearing."

"Howdy Goldy. My name's Rivers."

"Good to meet you. Dolf says you gonna break horses. I'm right proud you're here. Wouldn't missed what you did to Durham for the world."

"Thanks. Sorry about the tussle with Durham. He could have left it alone if he had wanted to."

"It ain't in him to leave anything alone. He does kinda pick who he bullys though. He ain't never tried it with me. I just mind my own business. I need the job."

"Well, I guess we'll see if he can leave it alone."

"He won't. You've called him a coward in front of all the men."

"He is a coward."

"You don't understand. I've seen him whip more than one man close to death with his bare hands."

"Bet he hit'em first and when they wasn't looking," Rivers said.

Goldy grinned from ear to ear. "You ain't no pilgrim are you?"

"Nope. I promise you the man will quit and beg when he faces somebody who will stand toe to toe with him."

"Kinda had that figured myself. Always felt if I ever had a run-in with him, I'd keep my eyes right on him. I'd never turn my back."

The two men talked on while Rivers stored his gear. They then went to the big room in the other bunkhouse where the hands ate. When they walked in it got quiet for a minute and then without a word being said to them the normal banter of a bunch of cow hands picked back up. Rivers cased the room and did not see Durham. The two moved to sit where they could see the door. Rivers led in that direction and Goldy laughed to himself.

The food came to the table and the men started helping their plates. A couple of the men introduced themselves to Rivers and it opened the floodgate of all the men around the table giving him their names.

A man named Utley spoke from down at the end of the table. "Better watch yourself Rivers. Durham told us all he was going to kill you."

Rivers looked up from his food and smiled. "Not unless he can talk ya'll into overpowering me and tie me to a pole."

They all laughed. They didn't really know this man, but they all took notice he wasn't scared.

"Don't take him lightly," an older man named Woods said. "He's as strong as a bull."

"You can relax for now," Red Beasley said with a chuckle. "Said he wasn't eating tonight. Got himself a terrible headache."

They all laughed and went back to eating. After they finished the meal, they sat around and talked for a couple of hours. Rivers mostly listened. He did answer a couple of questions about his horse. The men had seen War and wanted to know about him. Rivers did not tell them the entire story.

When they finally went to turn in, Goldy noticed how the new man placed his boots by the bunk and put his clothes so he could get in them quickly. His rifle was leaning against the wall in easy reach. When he slipped under the blanket, he took his knife with him. Goldy thought, a feller ought to be careful waking that man up.

10

Rivers was up before breakfast. He saddled his horse and led him to the holding pen where the young horses he was to break were held. He took his rope and walked inside to look them over. He settled on a mare and threw a loop over her head. She fought it for a little while and then followed Rivers as he led her through the gate and into the breaking corral. Once inside, the young mare fought against the rope and jumped all over the corral.

Rivers stood still, holding the rope firmly, and began to speak to the horse in a low soothing voice. She settled down after a while and he moved closer to rub her neck and shoulders. He continued to talk as he rubbed the tension out of the horse. After about ten minutes of this, he wrapped the rope around the pole in the center of the corral and left to bring his horse inside. Sitting atop War, he reached down and untied the rope from the pole and wrapped it around the saddle horn, leaving only about ten feet of lead for the mare. He nudged War through the gate and out into the ranch yard. Once out of the yard he kicked War into a trot, almost dragging the horse along.

When clear of the yard, he pushed War into a steady gallop. The young mare was having to run at a pretty good clip to keep up. After about ten minutes he pulled up and the young horse stood to his side, breathing heavily. Rivers swung down and walked over slowly. He rubbed the horses along the neck and shoulders for about a minute. Rivers thought, I want her to think it's her mothers tongue. Then he turned quickly, mounted up, and off they went again. His philosophy was to put the horse into controlled stress and make her believe he was the best friend she had. After about four of these running trips followed by tender rubbing, the horse developed a different attitude. As soon as he pulled War up, the mare would walk toward him anticipating the rubbing.

He walked War back into the ranch yard and led the young horse into the corral. The mare followed him all over the corral like a little puppy. He stopped periodically and rubbed her neck. He would turn away and she would follow. Every time he did this, the bond between them was strengthened.

Rivers got a bridle with a smooth bit off the corral fence and jangled it and rubbed it close to the horses' nose. He repeated it a few times and then gently put the bit in her mouth and raised the bridle over her ears. She didn't fight it at all. When it was on her, he rubbed her neck and shoulders for a while.

Satisfied she was calm, he began to rub her back gently and after a while with more pressure. He stopped now and then to rub her neck and face. The big test came when he pushed his chest up on her back and put his weight on her. Just for a moment. He slid back off and rubbed the tension out of her. It was getting easier for him to do. A matter of minutes later he was sitting on her back while leaning forward with his long arms to rub her neck. A gentle nudge had her walking around the corral carrying this new friend on her back.

Unnoticed by Rivers a crowd had gathered watching the entire episode. To see a man break a horse in such a gentle manner was foreign to them.

"Beats anything I've ever seen," one of them said. "Ain't even breakfast time yet and he's got a horse that ain't ever been touched by a man's hands eating outa his."

Dolf Freeman and Orvil Peters were standing on the porch of the main house watching the whole thing. Freeman had called his boss outside when he saw what was happening.

"The man's got a way with horses," Peters said.

"Sure does. Besides that, he's got a way with a lot of other things.

Wish you could have seen how he handled Durham."

"It ain't likely that a man like him is riding the grub line Dolf. There's more to him than that. Check him out and see what his game is."

"I plan on it."

"Good. Let's go down and eat breakfast with them," Peters said.

The cow hands were already around the table when Freeman and Peters arrived. The place was buzzing with talk of the new man and the way he broke the horse to ride. Everybody was in to it except Durham. He was sitting quietly in a brooding spirit. Rivers was the last to arrive. When he came in he walked to an empty chair by Durham and took a seat. He acted as if he had not even noticed the big man sitting beside him.

Durham had a knot in the middle of his forehead and a blue circle around it. They managed to eat breakfast without an exchange of words. When Durham stood up to leave, he broke the ice. He spoke to Rivers in a voice loud enough for everybody in the room to hear.

"When we get through work today, meet me in the corral where you tricked me yesterday. I got a whupping for you," Durham said with a sure and certain look on his face.

"I don't know when I'll get through. Why don't we just go on over there now," Rivers said casually, as if he didn't have a care in the world.

Durham was surprised. He hadn't figured on it working this way. He looked around a minute and said the only thing he could. "Suits me."

Durham started for the door and stopped suddenly. Rivers was talking.

"If you fellows don't mind, this is just between Durham and me. This needs to be a private thing."

Goldy had already slipped out when Durham first spoke and was hanging outside the door. When he heard Rivers tell the others to stay away, he hustled to the inside of the barn where he could see the corral through the cracks in the wall.

The men nodded their understanding about the fight being private and the two men walked out and headed for the corral. When they got inside, they stood close, facing each other.

"I'm gonna whup you good," Durham said. "You don't carry no gun and I ain't good with a knife, so I guess this is all I got." He held up his big fists, taunting Rivers.

"It's your choice," Rivers replied. "Let me get rid of this." He unbuckled the belt holding his knife and turned to walk toward the fence. He took one step and suddenly ducked and turned quickly to his left. He heard the swish of the big fist as it went over his head. He carried his turn all the way around and threw a wicked right that landed squarely on the wide open jaw of the big man. Rivers put his weight into the punch and rolled through it with his shoulder. Durham crumpled to the ground.

Durham rolled around on the ground for a while, groaning and trying to get up.

Rivers walked over and extended his hand. "Here. Let me help you."

Durham took his hand and stood on wobbly legs, trying to focus his eyes.

Rivers said, "Dolf Freeman spoke of firing you after our tussle yesterday. The way I figure it, you need the job. If you're willing, we'll forget this whole thing and get busy around here."

Durham was shocked. The man was actually trying to help him. "Seems fair to me," he said.

Rivers put out his hand and said, "Shake on it."

Durham shook his hand. They then walked side by side back to where the rest of the men were. When they walked in, everybody there was trying to size up what had happened. Nobody said a word.

After another cup of coffee, Rivers said, "Well, I've got horses to break." He stood and walked out.

After he was gone, Durham said, "I'm telling you all to leave that man alone. First off, he'd kill any one of you in a fair fight. Second, I'll kill you if you mess with him. He may be the only real man I've ever met."

Peters looked at Freeman and smiled. "You better get these men moving. We've got work to do."

The men stood and moved out to get busy. Goldy was standing by the corral when Rivers returned.

"Saw two amazing things already and the day is still young," Goldy said to Rivers.

"What'd you see," Rivers asked?

"Saw you break a horse by making her realize she was better off with you as a friend than being off by herself."

"Yep. That's the way it works. What else did you see?"

"Saw you do Durham the same way."

Rivers laughed and said, "My grandfather said it worked pretty good on kids too. I guess he was right. It sure worked on me."

11

The first few days on the Crooked Wind went by fast. Rivers was up to his neck in what he loved most. The young horses responded well to him and he had ten of the thirty wearing a saddle and comfortable with him on their backs. Not a single one had bucked. Each time he rode the back of a fresh broke horse, he did it without a saddle. It was really how he preferred to do all his riding. His journey into the white man's world made the saddle necessary. You could always tell more about your horse without a saddle. You could feel it when the horse became tense and the horse could feel it when you wanted something from him. The squeezing of the knees or a slight bump with the legs were good communications between a man and a horse.

The horses he was breaking would be working horses ridden by white men who knew little of the personalities of horses. It's rare to find a man who does. Rivers was taught much of what he knew by Red Wolf. The rest was the part you are born with. You either have it or you don't. He was proud he had it.

Rivers was between horses when Dolf Freeman walked over to the corral. Nobody else was around.

"Been watching you close, Rivers," he said. "You are mighty good with horses. Makes me wonder why you would be riding around looking for a job."

Rivers looked him in the eye and said, "If you are fishing in this stream, the best way to catch something is to come right out and ask. Otherwise, they ain't biting today."

Freeman grinned and said, "I was that obvious, huh. Okay, here goes. Who are you really and what is it you're up to?"

"Now, that's better," Rivers chuckled. "I really am who I say I am. What I'm up to is learning all I can about ranching. Some day I want to own a ranch and raise horses. I'm looking as I travel. I hope to find a good place to buy."

"Now I can believe that. I do admit you could do well with horses. To dream is one thing. To own a ranch is another. There's a lot more to ranching than raising cattle or horses. The business side of it is what's tough. Then there's the matter of money. It takes some money to buy a place. I don't see how you could manage that on a hired hand's wages."

"I've been saving up for a while and have a good start stored away in a bank back east."

"I figured there was more to you than the average feller riding through."

Rivers smiled and said, "If I'm going to get paid and add to my sack, then I've got some work to do. I better get back to these horses." With that, he walked over and swung a loop over the head of his next horse.

Freeman walked to the main house and went in to see Peters.

"Found out a little about our man Rivers. Seems he has his heart set on buying a ranch and raising horses."

"Does he know what it takes to buy and run a ranch?"

"Didn't seem to bother him none when I brought it up. Says he's been saving his money for a spell and has it in a bank back east somewhere."

"What about that. Do you believe him?"

"He's pretty sharp. He caught onto my prying real quick and told me to ask my questions straight out. Why, I can usually get one of these cow hands to spill his guts. Not him. He's wise beyond his years."

"Does he know anything about this area?"

"Don't believe so."

"Well, he's doing a good job. I've watched him too. Why don't you tell him I want him to eat supper with me here in the big house tomorrow night. I've got a hunch this man is the kind of fellow who will make a good stand in this land. I've seen a lot of people come through here who didn't have what it would take to make it. I believe he does. Maybe I can help him. I figure he's the kind who will leave his mark on the land."

"I'll do it," Freeman said as he left the house.

12

Rivers went to the main house a little before five o'clock in the afternoon two days later. He wasn't sure why Peters asked him to come for supper. He had not spoken to the man other than a casual hello since he had been on the Crooked Wind. All the men seemed to like Peters and he thought the boss probably just wanted to get to know him better. He walked up on the porch and knocked on the door. He had taken time to wash up a bit and change clothes.

Peters came to the door and invited Rivers in.

"Let's go in here and talk a spell while they are getting the food on the table," Peters said as he led the way into a room with four big stuffed rawhide chairs. They took a seat.

"Dolf tells me you've got your mind set on buying a ranch and raising horses," Peters said to begin the conversation.

"Yes. I hope to. I've always wanted to do it and I'm going to be looking for a place I can afford," Rivers replied.

"You've got a way with horses. I've been watching your work. I can see you do enjoy it. By the way, that big black stallion of yours would sire some good stock."

"I'm counting on it. Do you know of any places around here I might check out?"

"That's one of the reasons I wanted to talk to you. I don't usually talk my personal business with people I don't know. Do you think you can keep our conversation just between the two of us?"

"Mr. Peters, you really don't know me. If you did, you would know who I am is more important to me than anything else. I was raised that way by my grandfather. I don't talk a lot and I sure don't talk about things I've made a promise to keep. I promise you our conversation will be between just the two of us."

"Good. I am just about as good with people as you are with horses. I had you pegged to be a man you could trust. Let me tell you a little of my story. I moved out here from Georgia in eighteen nineteen. The government built the fort here in eighteen seventeen. Some of the government officials back in Georgia talked me into coming out here to start an operation to provide meat for the soldiers as well as re-mounts for the cavalry. At the time this area was at the edge of the movement west and I thought it would be a good opportunity for me. My kids were gone and settled. Me and the wife came out here and bought the land. I had some brood mares and some cattle driven out here to get started. Most of my cattle were of European blood. I have since crossed them with a few longhorns brought up from down south in the Texas Republic. I've built a good ranch and have a profitable business. My wife died on me about three years back and it ain't been the same since. I'm telling you all this to say I might be interested in selling the Crooked Wind."

"That is interesting. By the way, I came out from Georgia," Rivers said.

"Did you really. What part?"

"I was raised up in north Georgia."

"If that don't beat all."

They were interrupted by a small man who came into the room and announced that supper was on the table. They followed him to the kitchen and took a seat around a small table.

They helped their plates with beef and beans with plenty of fresh baked bread. They continued to talk as they ate.

Rivers said, "We'll talk about Georgia later. Let's talk about the ranch."

"Suits me. There's one thing I feel like I need to tell you before we go a ways on down the road. When I came here, I already told you, this place was on the edge of the movement west. I wouldn't want you to consider buying this place without knowing that could all change. To be honest, the edge has already moved. The Santa Fe trail is opening up big time in Missouri since the Mexicans are allowing trade to come from this way. They and the Spanish kept it all coming from Mexico until the Spanish hightailed it. Now the Mexicans are realizing there is a lot of profit and better goods for them to have coming from us. They are also shipping things back on some of the wagons to be sold here. I'm saying all this to point out I don't know how long the government will keep the fort open. There ain't a need for it like there once was. If it closed down, your market for the sale of beef and horses would dry up."

Rivers was amazed this man was telling him things to actually make the sale of his ranch look unattractive. And he was a white man. He thought, I wonder if Red Wolf would let this man wash and wrap his tail.

"I appreciate you telling me all this. You could have offered me the ranch without saying a word."

"You spoke of the raising your grandfather gave you. I had a pretty good raising too. I might own more than the man down the road, but if he don't respect me, then I figure I have failed. If you were to buy this place, I would want you to respect me long after I'm gone."

"That's fair enough. I need to tell you some things about myself. It might change how you feel about selling me the ranch. Like you mentioned earlier, this will have to be just between the two of us."

"I can handle that," Peters replied.

"The name I grew up with was Tse-quo-ni. I am a Cherokee warrior from the high mountains where the sun rises. My father was a white man. I never accepted the white man's ways and because of it I was raised by my Cherokee grandparents. I escaped when the government moved my people from their homeland. I am determined to live my life free and at the mercy of no man, red or white. My grandfather taught me to look for people I could trust. He taught me to trust white men who were men of honor. I judge you to be that kind of man, or I would never be sharing my past with you."

"I am a man of honor and I admire your courage. I probably would have done the same thing. It changes nothing about my feelings for you," Peters said.

"Because of what has happened, I need a place to call mine quickly. I have a sister who was removed from Georgia with my family. My mother died before the journey could begin. I promised myself I would get my sister and give her a life other than what the government will give her. I plan to go soon and take her away from the place they call the Indian Territory."

"You are not all that far from it," Peters said.

"I know and it is why I am here."

"You do not have to buy my ranch to have a place to bring her. I would welcome her to stay here until you decide to leave," Peters added.

"I don't know how long I will need to be here and owning your ranch would give me the means of continuing another search. I am also looking for a man named McCloud who supposedly raises horses somewhere out west. He left out of Georgia over twenty years ago. Have you ever heard of such a name?"

Peters thought for a moment, and then said, "Yes. I was at Fort Smith once when a man described a horse to be a McCloud horse. I asked how he knew. I was looking at the horse as we spoke and he told me there were no other horses that could match a McCloud horse. It was a beautiful animal. I wish now I had pursued the conversation for your benefit. Why are you looking for McCloud?"

"The answer to that is something I do not need to tell you now. Perhaps some day I will. How long ago was your encounter with the man who talked about the McCloud horse?"

"It was probably four years ago, maybe five."

"So there is a McCloud somewhere out here who raises horses."

"Must be. Rivers, you have spoken nothing of money. Are you in a financial position to buy a ranch. I could help you some in delaying payment for part of the purchase if it was necessary. I will need part of the price for my own personal reasons," Peters said.

"I have the money, although we have not discussed a price. I must warn you, I am a fierce trader." Rivers smiled at Peters.

"Are you telling me you are carrying around enough money to buy this ranch?"

"No. I have a letter signed by Amos Griggs of Gainesville, Georgia, and his bank stating I have money deposited in his bank to cover any business transaction I make."

"No kidding. Amos Griggs. Know him. Matter of fact he was one of the last people I talked to when I left out of Georgia. He handles some of my business back there. He's one fine man."

"He is the white man my grandfather taught me to trust. I think my grandfather would have trusted you too."

"That makes me proud, Rivers. Do you want to talk money tonight?"

"No. We will be able to come to an agreement. How soon do you want to leave here?"

"I'm not in any hurry. I sure don't want to travel in the winter. The main thing I want to do is get back home and get settled in somewhere before I get too old. I might even find me a good woman to spend the rest of my life with. There ain't none in these parts."

"Then why don't we agree tonight to make a deal for your ranch. When I finish with the horses, I can go and get my sister. We will have plenty of time to make the other decisions after that."

"That sounds fine to me," Peters said.

"You understand why I don't want what I'm doing talked around. I could get in trouble with the government. I plan on bringing her out of there with no trail to follow and no smoke to lead anybody here. My sister speaks English well and by the time I get her into some white peoples' clothes nobody would ever guess she was an Indian. She is only fourteen. You will enjoy getting to meet her."

"It will be good to have a child around the house again," Peters said.

"So, we will just go along as if nothing has changed and we will tell the others when the time is right. Okay?"

"Okay."

"There is one other thing. I've noticed one of the hands on the ranch everybody calls the Breed. Is he Indian?"

"He is a half breed Kiowa. His Indian name is Night Hawk. Me and Dolf call him Midnight. He is a good man and a good hand. Why do you ask?"

"If it is all-right, I want him to help me with the horses. I've watched him with his horse and he knows horses. I also want to get to know him. The Cherokee language is unlike any plains Indians. It might be of use to me to learn to speak the Kiowa language. I don't know where my search for the man named McCloud will lead me. It might help me on down the road."

"I'll see to it."

They talked on a while and then Rivers left to get some sleep. He had a busy day coming up. The sooner he got the horses ready, the sooner he could head out for his sister. He lay in the bunk before he drifted off and thought back over his conversation with Peters. Could it be there were more good white men than he realized.

13

The next morning when Rivers went to the corral to begin his day he found Night Hawk waiting for him. The day would mark the beginning of a long time of constant companionship.

"They told me you wanted me to help you with the horses," Night Hawk said.

"That's right. I've noticed you have a way with horses. I figured it was your Kiowa blood. I hear your people have a history of raising good horses," Rivers replied.

"Kiowa horses are some of the best on the plains. I was around them from the time I could walk. Most white people treat me like the Kiowa treated me. My mixed blood caused me to feel unwanted there and here."

"Does Mr. Peters make you feel unwanted?"

"No. He has treated me like a man. Freeman does too."

"I will tell you something if you can keep my word," Rivers said.

"I am a man of honor," Night Hawk replied.

"I am of mixed blood too. My mother was Cherokee and my father was a white man. I consider myself Cherokee. I am just learning to trust some white men."

Night Hawk looked at Rivers closely and said, "I have known it. What is your Indian name?"

"Tse-quo-ni. It means Rivers in the white tongue. Mr. Peters told me your name is Night Hawk. Is that true?"

"Yes. My mother was Kiowa and my father was a white mountain man I never knew. It did not bother me until I got old enough to understand the taunts of others my age and older people. They called me white dog. When it became unbearable, I left. I was not old enough to become a warrior at the time. I learned to take care of myself and make it in the white man's world. It is hard at times. I've learned to hide my anger. If I did what I wanted to, the white man would probably hang me."

"You said you had known I had Indian blood. Does it show I am Indian?"

"It does to me. I said nothing because if you are ashamed of it, then I have no respect for you."

"I am proud to be Cherokee. I hate my white blood. I only keep it quiet because the government is moving all of my people to the Indian Territory. I escaped before they took my people captive. My reason for asking you to keep my word has nothing to do with my pride in being a Cherokee. My sister was moved to the Indian Territory and I plan to go take her away from there. I cannot allow anything to happen that would direct attention to me right now."

"So, we are brothers."

"Yes. We are both Indians. Right?"

"Right. I have heard of your people from old stories. You were once strong. Then you became like the white people."

"The Cherokee people did. I never accepted the white man's ways. I only do it now because my future is in the white man's world. I will always be Cherokee."

"Why are you here? Is it because of your sister?"

"Yes. When the horses are broken and ready for delivery to the Army, I will go and take her away from the Indian Territory. I have spoken with Mr. Peters and he will allow me to bring her here."

"He is a good man. He is the only white man who has treated me like a man and not like a dog."

"You speak as if you have bad feelings of the Kiowa people. Is it true?"

"No. The Kiowa are fierce warriors in battle and ride the horse with skill. I would still be living with them if the white blood in me had died. The Kiowa never accepted me and banished my mother to a life of cruelty. They made her work like an animal until her death. I left before they killed me. With all of that, I still take pride in my Kiowa blood."

"I understand. It is so with me as well. I would like you to help me learn to speak the Kiowa language. Would you help me learn?"

"Yes. Why do you want to speak my language?"

"After I get my sister away from the government, I have another job to do that I will tell you about later. Knowing your language might help me. Your people still live on the plains don't they?"

"Yes. I will help you learn to speak my language."

The two men went to work breaking the horses. Every spare minute they had, when no one else could hear, was spent discussing the Kiowa language. Rivers was a quick learner and soon they spoke in Kiowa as easily as they did in the white man's tongue. The weather grew cold and the horses were getting closer to being ready to deliver to the Army.

During the days of working with the horses, an amazing circle of friendship began to form. It was almost coincidental at first, but then soon it became apparent as a matter of choice. Roscoe Durham, Goldy Sharp, Night Hawk, and Rivers began to sit together when eating, talk together after supper and into the night, and obviously began to keep an eye out for each other when around the ranch or riding out onto the area around it. It was an unlikely friendship. Durham had been thoroughly humbled by Rivers, but yet had earned his respect and loyalty. Goldy, the quiet strong man, had respected Rivers from the first. Night Hawk was first tied to Rivers by their common Indian blood, but the fact Rivers had singled him out to help with the horses brought his respect for the new arrival at the Crooked Wind to the surface. The unlikely aspect of their friendship was not their respect for Rivers. They began to respect and depend on each other. Goldy liked the new and humbled version of Durham. Durham admitted he had never bullied Goldy because he knew the man wouldn't take it. Night Hawk accepted the two men when they treated him with respect and made him believe they would trust him to cover their backs under any circumstance. Who would have ever thought such a varied combination of strong men would give birth to a coalition of loyalty to each other. None of the three had the slightest inclination of Rivers' financial power and soon to come to pass plans to own the Crooked Wind. But Rivers took notice of them in a different way. They would be men he could count on to build his life among the white men. He had no doubt Durham and Goldy would accept his Indian blood when he chose to tell them. They had readily accepted the same in Night Hawk.

The day finally came. Upon Rivers request, the foursome drove the band of thirty horses to Fort Smith and turned them over to the Army. Afterwards, sitting around a table in a café, Rivers told Durham and Goldy about his Indian heritage. He also told them of his plans to go for his sister. He chose to wait about telling them of his plans to buy the ranch. All three men wanted to accompany him into the Indian Territory and help him find his sister. Rivers thanked them and explained it would be much easier if he did it alone. They understood and agreed to let him go alone. Their feeling and loyalty was expressed best by Goldy, who closed the subject as they saddled up to head back to the ranch.

"One thing you need to know before you leave to get your sister. We'll give you two weeks to get back. If you ain't here by then, we'll be on our way to get you," Goldy said.

The other two smiled and nodded their agreement.

14

Rivers left out at first light. He was trailing a saddle horse for his sister and a pack horse loaded with food, blankets, and a winter coat for Mary. He had spoken with Mr. Peters at length about his journey and inquired of his knowledge of the Indian Territory, specifically the Neosho Creek area. Peters told him to travel due north for about three days until he came to a settlement surrounding a series of hot springs. Then he was to turn directly west and would come up on the Neosho about two days into the territory.

Rivers knew he would be fortunate to find his sister without a lot of difficulty. He had an urgency about him for two reasons. It was continually getting colder and he wanted to get her back to the ranch before the brutal cold hit. He was also concerned about how his sister might be treated after his mother's death. He had very little trust in Franklin Ross.

He rode steadily north and encountered no difficulty. He was on the trail before daylight and stopped with the final light each day. He came to the settlement around the springs on the third day and skirted it without making any contact. On the fifth day he started seeing groups of Indians camped along a small creek. He pulled back to some high ground and glassed the area. He saw no familiar face. Some of the Indians were living in small cabins and others were sleeping under makeshift coverings while they were busy building more cabins.

Staying away from the congested area he continued north, stopping to glass each gathering of Indians he found along the creek. He worked through seven such groups and was coming into late afternoon when he spotted the eighth in the distance. He rode into some brush on a small knoll and crawled to the edge to glass this one.

Immediately, upon his first peep through the glass, he saw someone he knew. It was Franklin Adair. He and other familiar faces were seated outside a small log cabin. They seemed to be in deep conversation. Rivers figured it to be a tribal talk of some kind.

As he watched them, he noticed movement beside the cabin and shifted his glass to see his sister busy at a large pot with a small fire. His heart jumped. Mary was alive. He looked her over good. She looked thin and her clothes were obviously too big and tattered.

He watched as she nursed the fire beneath the pot and occasionally stirred it's contents. She was probably cooking a stew.

Rivers mind drifted back to the day Mary was born. He had always called her Star. His mother was so proud to have a daughter. She had grown to be a beautiful girl. He continued to watch her and thought, the white man has tried to break her spirit. They failed. He was watching a young girl who had been accustomed to comfort doing what she must to survive. She held her head high. It made him proud of her.

He moved into a cautious mode and slipped back into the brush. He ground hitched the horses and nestled into the brush to eat some jerked beef. After a spell he crawled back to the edge and studied the layout.

There were about twenty of the small cabins gathered in a single clump. He glassed upstream and downstream. He could make out the smoke of other fires in both directions. He went back to the house where he saw his sister. It sat closer to the creek than the others. That would be an advantage. He figured his best bet in and out would be by the stream. How he would get her out of the cabin was another matter. He would just have to figure that out when he got close. Maybe he could get lucky.

As soon as it became dark Rivers moved out on foot. He walked slowly and held low to the ground. His route took him about two hundred paces upstream from Mary's cabin. When he came to the stream, he reached down and felt the water. It was cold. He forced himself to wade out into the stream and stopped when the water was waist deep. All he had to defend himself was his knife. His rifle and pistols were with the horses. He didn't want to get into a shooting war with these people. In reality, they were his people. He hoped to snatch Mary and get away without being seen.

After a few seconds of adjusting to the cold water, Rivers lowered his body until only his head was above water. He lifted his feet and let the current take him downstream. He maneuvered himself to the west bank and floated quietly. In a matter of seconds he anchored himself to the bottom about twenty paces from Mary's cabin. He could hear voices. He saw no movement. He decided to wait. He didn't know how long he could last in the water. It was awfully cold.

A little while later the door to her cabin swung open and the lamp light spilled out into the dark. Rivers crouched as low as he could get and keep his head above water. Someone walked out the door and went around the side of the cabin. Rivers had spotted a wood pile there earlier. He had to get closer.

Stepping quietly out of the water, he moved like a cougar stalking it's prey. A few quick steps covered the space between the steam and the cabin. His eyes never left the person gathering the wood. Somewhere in the process he became certain it was Mary. He would know her on the darkest night.

She was busy stacking the wood to take inside when strong arms grabbed her and a hand was pressed over her mouth. She tried to scream. Her eyes were wild as she tried to free herself. She caught sight of her assailant about the same time he whispered for her to be quiet. She turned and threw her arms around Rivers as soon as he released his grip.

"Rivers. I've been so worried about you," she whispered. "What are you doing here?"

"I've come for you. I want you to come live with me," Rivers replied.

"If they catch you, they will make you stay here," she said.

"They don't have enough soldiers to keep me here. I am going to live free and I want you to live free. I promised mother I would come for you. Will you slip out later and come with me?" Rivers asked.

"Yes. I hate it here."

"We have much to talk about, but it must wait." Rivers pointed to the stream. "When they are asleep, sneak out and meet me there. Don't worry about bringing anything. Dress warm. I will be waiting." Rivers then slipped back into the darkness.

Mary loaded her arms with wood and went inside.

The cabin was quiet and the night young when Rivers saw the shadowy figure moving toward him. Without saying a word he took her hand and led her across the stream and to the place where he left the horses. He dug out some dry pants and a heavy coat for her to put on. He then lifted her into the saddle and rode north east for a while until he found some rocky ground where tracks would be hard to follow. He then headed due east. Rivers wanted distance between them and the village by daylight.

They rode through the night without talking. Rivers was proud of how Mary handled the horse and kept up the pace. He estimated they had traveled over twenty miles by sunrise. They topped out on a rise and Rivers stopped to check out his back trail. He saw no sign of being followed. Certain they were safe, he led them down the other side and back into some thick pines where they would be shielded from any travelers along the way. He quickly hitched the horses and had a small fire going. Mary fell in to cooking bacon and coffee. Rivers stripped the horses and let them roll before hitching them in close.

They began to talk as they ate.

"Tell me about mother. Was her death easy?" Rivers asked.

"Yes. She was so weak when they took us. They put her in a wagon to help them move quickly. We did not get to the landing where they held the boats before she died. The others in the wagon said she just stopped breathing. I was walking close by, but I could not see her. They stopped the wagon to tell us she was dead. We buried her beside the road." Mary looked at Rivers with sad eyes. "They did not give us long to bury her. I did your crying and sang your death song for you at her grave."

Rivers reached over and took her hand. "Thank you. You know

she had great dreams for you. She told me once you were the smartest Cherokee she knew." Rivers laughed. "It made me angry when she said it. Now I agree with her," he said.

"She always told me to never settle for a life that would not bring me happiness. For some reason I never felt like mother was completely happy. I knew she was happy when she was with me or you. It seemed like the rest of the time she did what she had to do simply because she had to do it. Did you ever feel that way?" Mary asked.

"Yes. I must tell you of my last conversation with mother," Rivers said.

He allowed the story to unfold just as he had heard it from her lips. He told her about Matthew McCloud being his father. He told her of his mother's love for McCloud and how she had married Mary's father as a means of avoiding embarrassment. He then led her each step along the path he had followed until the moment he had taken her hand to lead her away from the Cherokee people. Mary sat quietly during the long discourse and did not interrupt Rivers.

When he finished, he sat looking into her eyes. He knew she would have questions.

"So we have the same mother and different fathers?" she asked.

"Yes. That does not make us weak or distant. The Cherokee blood of our mother won the battle for both of us while we were in her womb. We came out of her Cherokee. The other two did not. So the white man did not win. We are closer than a brother and sister. We carry the blood of a proud woman who locked our lives together."

"The McCloud man, your father, does not know about you?"

"No. And he is not my father. He is but a man. Mother loved him and asked me to speak to him for her if I ever find him. I will wait to do that. A part of me hates him. A part of me wants to see what caused my mother to love him so much. You must help me keep the secret until I am ready to talk with him."

"I can keep your secret."

"Mary, we will have much time for talking. I want to know everything about your life since you left our mountains. First, we must sleep a little and get back on the trail. It is possible someone will be following us."

Rivers put out the fire and sprinkled dirt on it to keep it from smoldering. They rolled up in blankets and slept until the sun was in the middle of the sky. In a matter of minutes they were packed and riding east.

The time on the trail gave them opportunity to talk. Rivers learned of the many who died before the river travel began and others who died en route or soon after arriving in the Indian Territory. Rivers purposely did not talk about his dislike for Franklin Adair. He loved his sister too much. He would never ask her to dislike her father. However, he did sense in Mary, without words spoken, that her single source of life, pride, and courage was her mother. Rivers could understand. She had been his too.

15

They rode into the settlement around the hot springs late on the second day. He saw one sign reading Siloam Springs and figured it to be the name. There were about fourteen buildings housing businesses and a number of dwellings back from the springs. Rivers stopped to get a few supplies. He also wanted to get Mary some new clothes. She looked every bit the Indian and he wanted to disguise it as much as possible. He also had a bath, a couple of good meals, and a bed on his mind.

Rivers led Mary into a dry goods store at the end of a makeshift street and told her to find some clothes. She rummaged through the jeans and shirts, holding them up for Rivers to approve. He went to a rack holding some women's dresses and held up one.

"I don't need that," she said.

"You never know. I'm sure the boys will come calling when I get you back to the ranch," Rivers replied with a laugh.

"They'll lose their hair too," she said.

"I want you to have it."

The dress was made of a beautiful blue material with three circles of lace around the bottom. Mary held it up and smiled .

"I like it. We'll get it too. Get yourself some boots and a hat. If you're going to be a ranch hand, you've got to look like one," Rivers said.

Rivers paid for the things and they were out the door in less than thirty minutes. He led the way to a saloon with a small café. He carried the new purchases under his arm. A small sign said you could get hot food inside. Hot food was what he wanted.

They walked in and took a seat at a small rough-sawed table over in the corner. A few people were seated around eating. Rivers ordered for both and they enjoyed a big bowl of beef stew and cornbread. It was so good Rivers ordered a second bowl. When they finished they sat drinking coffee and chatting about the rest of the trip. Rivers told her of his plans to buy the ranch and she could plan on having a real home. She asked about where he got the money to buy the ranch and he explained about the gold. Mary was astounded. Her brother was rich.

As they talked, a rough looking gent walked over to their table.

"Got you a mighty purty little squaw," he said. "Had me one a while back. You wouldn't want to get shed of her would you?"

Mary tensed and was about to speak when she read Rivers eyes. They were telling her to be quiet. Rivers continued to sip his coffee and ignored the man. The stranger reached over and ran his hand over the lace on Mary's new dress.

"Sure would like to see what that looks like with a warm pair of legs in it," he said.

The room had grown quiet. What happened next was so quick it caught everyone, especially the stranger, by surprise.

Rivers stood up in a flash and when he reached full height he already had the man by the shirt with his left hand and his right hand held the razor sharp blade of his knife against the man's throat.

"You have offended my sister," Rivers spoke in a low voice. "Now there was a time when I'd a slit your throat without talking." He looked at Mary and said, "Would you mind waiting outside?"

Mary stood and walked quickly out the door. Rivers then turned his attention back to the wide-eyed man who was leaning against the knife blade as gently as he could. Sweat was rolling down his face.

"You say you want to see what this dress looks like with a warm pair of legs in it. Get your clothes off and put it on," Rivers said.

The man squirmed out of his clothes. He never got far enough away from the knife blade to stop feeling it. The people began to giggle as the spectacle developed

They broke out in belly laughs as the man tried to get the dress over his head and shoulders. He finally got most of it on and stood there looking like an idiot.

Rivers stood in front of him and looked deep into his eyes. "It looks real good on you, but I bought it for her to wear. Now we are going to spend the night over at the boarding place and plan on leaving early in the morning. I want this dress ironed so it don't have one wrinkle in it. I'll pick it up when I come over for breakfast in the morning. Have we got a deal?"

The man nodded. Rivers turned, picked up the other clothes and walked out. He could still hear the roar of laughter as they walked into the bath and board house.

The next morning the dress was waiting for him, ironed to perfection. The man who ran the place told him the other fellow's name was Rod Shule. He had left the dress along with a message.

"Said your breakfast was already paid for and said for me to tell you he deserved what he got," the man said.

Rivers and Mary ate breakfast and walked out to their horses. The man who delivered the message followed them out and said, "Wouldn't take nothing for what you did to old Rod. He's had it coming. He'll take a long time to live that down."

Rivers smiled, stepped into the saddle, and they rode out of town.

16

They rode onto the Crooked Wind ranch three days later. Roscoe Durham, Goldy, and Night Hawk were happy to see them. Mr. Peters came out along with all the men who were around the ranch house at the time. Rivers swung down and helped his sister off her horse.

"Men, I want you to meet my sister," Rivers said. "This is Mary."

They all introduced themselves and welcomed her to the ranch. She was shy and did not like all the attention.

"It's a good thing you got back when you did," Goldy said. "We were heading out tomorrow to look for you."

"I appreciate your concern. We made it fine and as far as I know everything is okay," Rivers said.

"Mary, I have a room up at the house waiting for you. I would be pleased to have you stay there," Mr. Peters said.

"I would like that, but I don't want any special treatment," Mary said.

"It won't be special. You'll just be one of the crowd and there will be plenty for you to do," Peters replied.

"I would be pleased to help," she said.

"Fine. Goldy, why don't you take her to the house and I have a few things I need to talk to Rivers about," Peters said.

Goldy led the pack horse toward the ranch house and escorted Mary in that direction. The other men left Rivers and Mr. Peters alone.

"I'm glad you were able to get her out of the territory," Peters said.

"I don't think we were trailed. You never know. If anybody shows up here I'll need your help," Rivers said.

Peters laughed. "That's not a problem. As of right now she's my granddaughter and I'd like to see anybody take her away from here."

"I owe you. I appreciate what you are doing for me," Rivers replied.

"Oh I ain't doing nothing. I have some other information for you. There was a man at the Fort who was looking to buy some horses. I met him while you were gone. He was riding one of them McCloud horses we talked about. We struck a deal for ten of my young mares. I asked him where he got the horse and he told me he bought him off McCloud. It seems McCloud has a horse operation in New Mexico. The gent was full of talk and I just listened. He told me McCloud got his land the same way he acquired his. Seems McCloud was in strong with the Spanish and got a land grant from them. Said it grew out of a relationship McCloud's father had with the Spanish big dogs back in Texas. This fellow said he got his land the same way."

"Did he say what the McCloud man's name was," Rivers asked?

"Said it was Matt McCloud. His horse operation is not all that far from the gent's place. His is up in the Colorado territory. He said he would love to have bought the mares from McCloud, but he was asking too much for them. His stallion is a McCloud horse and he wants to raise some good stock off him."

"What was this man's name," Rivers asked?

"Wilson Fennel. We struck a deal and he's already paid me for the horses along with enough to cover me delivering them to him after winter breaks," Peters said. "He left out about a week ago heading back to his place."

"Well what about that. Seems like I am not having to do a lot of searching to find this man," Rivers said.

"I figured you might want to take your friends and deliver the horses to Fennel. It would be a good chance for you to find out more and maybe even get down that way," Peters said. "When winter breaks I want to head back east. Mary would be safe here until you get back. We can finalize the sale of the ranch and you can call all the shots."

"It sounds good to me. You give me some time to mull it over and I'll share it with the boys when the time is right. I don't want anybody knowing about me buying the place until I'm ready," Rivers said.

They walked on up to the house and made sure Mary had gotten settled in.

Winter came with a full blast of cold wind out of the northwest. It blew every day and made the work around the ranch tough. Rivers fell in with the other hands and did his share. Mary made the best of her new home and carried her share of the work around the house. Never far from Rivers mind was the encounter certain to occur with Matthew McCloud. His dislike for the man had not diminished one bit.

17

Rivers left the Crooked Wind and headed toward Colorado the first full week of moderate temperatures. He counted on more cold weather over the first few days of travel. The worst of winter was over. He left with a vivid picture in his mind of a teary eyed baby sister trying to be big. His last words to her was a promise to return for her as soon as possible.

The winter on the Crooked Wind gave Rivers the time to make preparation for the future. The ranch was now his. After the initial shock, the ranch hands took the news of his ownership well. They all respected the horse wrangler turned ranch owner.

Dolf Freeman was left in charge of running the ranch. Rivers, with Peters' approval, had brought Freeman into the deal when he purchased the ranch. Rivers made him owner of a quarter of the ranch and Freeman would work out his part of the purchase price. With Freeman there, the day to day work of the ranch would not change. He knew all the details of selling the horses and buying anything they needed. He also had accepted the responsibility of caring for Mary in Rivers absence. Rivers trusted him and Mary loved him like a grandfather. Rivers ultimate plan was to purchase another ranch further west and both would focus on raising horses with two markets.

Peters was to leave the Crooked Wind a couple of days after Rivers. Peters would get the bulk of his money from Amos Griggs when he got to Gainesville, Georgia. He was also to give Griggs directions to the Crooked Wind and tell him to deliver the mares he owed Rivers as soon as possible. If everything worked out, he could bring both Mary and the young mares west at the same time.

Peters had given Rivers directions to the Fennel ranch. He was to follow the Arkansas until it swung almost due north. Leaving it there, he was to follow a northwest direction until he hit the Arkansas again. It seemed the Arkansas made a large loop and the cross country leg would save him a lot of time. When he got back on the Arkansas, he was to follow it almost to the high mountains. Once there, he was to go south until he hit the Purgatoire River. Fennel's place, the Broken Wheel ranch, lay north of the Purgatoire and included the land up against the river for a number of miles.

Rivers and his friends went due west off the Crooked Wind until they came up on the Arkansas. Durham and Goldy were each trailing a line of five mares. Rivers and Night Hawk led pack horses. Rivers was in the lead and Night Hawk brought up the rear.

They would be traveling through dangerous territory and ultimately have three different tribes of Southern Plains Indians to contend with. Rivers felt comfortable with his friends. He reflected on the three men he had allowed to become close to him. Durham would charge Hell with nothing but his bare hands. Goldy was so smooth and secure in his own ability that Hell would stop in it's tracks and consider the options before taking him on. Night Hawk could be in and out of Hell without anybody knowing it and they would find the Devil with his throat cut the next day. Rivers chuckled to himself and thought, along with them, I'm the worst dream Hell could have. I think we'll be all right.

18

The journey west was not easy. First came the dense woodlands. The trees were so thick you could be on top of somebody before you knew it. Then came the rolling hills with broken areas of trees and sparse vegetation. An entire Kiowa war party could be just over the hill and you wouldn't know it. Finally the flat endless plains fell before them. The plains were marked with knobs of high ground like someone had piled up enough dirt and rocks to break the flat surface. They were laced with arroyos that followed no certain direction. You could cross the same one five times before you figured out how to go around it. This was all new to Rivers. Night Hawk was a big help because he had seen the area before.

Rivers and his men had two possessions the Indians cherished. Horses and firearms were a treasure to the plains Indians. They were able to avoid the Indians for the most part by being careful. They rode far enough away from the Arkansas to stay out of sight. The river would attract other travelers. They did not want their presence known to Indians or whites. When they stopped overnight, they withdrew to the place with the most cover and gave care to erase their signs leading to the camp. Fires were used sparingly and always before it grew dark. The horses were kept in close and one of the four was awake throughout each night.

Rivers or Night Hawk always rode out early before breaking camp and scouted the first few miles in front of them. They usually watered their animals at the river after they had been on the trail a while and well before they turned into a campsite in the evening. When they did break camp, one of them would remain behind in a concealed position to see if they were being followed. This saved their bacon one morning after leaving an overnight camp on the plains.

Night Hawk had stayed behind on this particular morning. He caught up to the others about an hour out of camp. He was in a full run when he pulled up beside Rivers.

"A party of Comanches came into our camp soon after we left. They looked around for signs and now they are on our trail," Night Hawk said.

"How many," Rivers asked?

"Ten."

"What kind of weapons do they have?"

"I saw no rifles," Night Hawk said. "Only bows."

"Then let's keep moving until we find the right place to greet them," Rivers said.

They rode on a couple of miles and came to a place where the plains dropped down about five feet in a gradual decent. You could look ahead and see where it rose back up about a mile in front of them.

"This is it," Rivers said. "Durham, take all the horses on down hill about two hundred paces and gather them up close so you can control them. You'll still be close enough for us to cover you if they flank us."

Durham took the horses and in no time had them circled tight around him. Rivers, Goldy, and Night Hawk stepped back from the horizon of their low spot far enough to be able to stand and barely look over the top. From there they could watch their back trail without being seen. The Comanches came into view about twenty minutes later with a trail of dust rising up behind them.

"If it comes to shooting, I will face them and the two of you cover the sides. We will all fire on them before they split. We won't shoot unless we have to," Rivers said.

They were coming closer at a gallop. Rivers marveled at their horsemanship and lean muscles glistening in the early morning sun. He thought, I could easily have been a part of them in another time and place.

The Comanches were startled to see three men who seemed to rise up from the ground. They pulled up immediately about twenty-five paces from them.

Their leader spoke, "Horses...guns we want. You go."

"No. You go," Rivers said.

"We take horses and guns. Kill you," the Indian said.

"I am Tse-quo-ni, Cherokee warrior from the high mountains where the sun appears. Our Great Spirit has promised me this day. He promised me I would count coup on a Comanche warrior. He has sent you," Rivers said.

The Indian looked around at his companions and they all laughed.

"How? There are more of us," the Indian said.

"There are three of us. We have nine guns. You will all die here today. I choose you to be the first to die," Rivers replied.

The Indians spoke among themselves. Rivers seized the opportunity and continued talking.

"You must choose to die here or live to talk around your campfire tonight. This is not about bravery. I know the Comanche is a fierce warrior. So is the Cherokee. I would like to sit by your fire and tell my story. I cannot. I must take these horses to their owner. If you choose to live, I will leave coffee and tobacco to honor your bravery. If you choose to die, then let it begin."

After a few minutes of conversation, accented with gestures and obvious changes in facial expressions, the leader said, "We choose to honor the Cherokee warrior by letting him live. Go."

Rivers chuckled at their ability to turn the tables and he replied with a raised hand, "Thank you. I accept the honor of the great Comanche warrior."

Rivers spoke in a whisper to Night Hawk, "Go fish out some tobacco and coffee from our pack and leave it on the ground. Tell Durham to start out with the horses and walk our mounts back here."

Night Hawk left immediately and was back in a few minutes with the horses. They mounted up and Rivers gave a final wave of the hand to the Indians as they turned and rode off to catch up with Durham. They kept a close watch behind them and saw the wary Comanches ride up to their cache when they were well out of range. Night Hawk stayed behind as they passed over the horizon. He would watch their back trail until he was sure they were no longer followed.

Night Hawk rode into their camp a while after dark and reported the Comanches had left their trail. After he ate, they talked of the encounter. When Rivers left to walk away from the fire to listen to the night sounds, the other men discussed the way he handled the band of Comanches.

"He's one smart feller," Goldy said. "Not many people could have talked their way out of that mess."

"I've got a feeling we are going to learn a lot more from him," Durham answered. "It makes me mighty proud to ride with him. He could have cut loose shooting and there's no telling how it would have ended up."

The talking died down and they rolled up in their blankets.

19

Two weeks followed without incident. The shock of Rivers' life occurred about mid-morning of a hot day. The group of travelers topped a small rise in the plains and saw the horizon blanketed with a sight foreign to his eyes. From south to north, as far as the eyes could see, a wall of mountains shot halfway to the sky. He pulled up and set there amazed.

"I felt the same way the first time I saw them," Night Hawk said as he stopped beside Rivers.

"They make the high mountains of my homeland seem small," Rivers said. "How far away are they?"

"We will ride many days before we reach them," Night Hawk replied.

They rode six days before they were close enough to the mountains to make out their detailed dimensions. They became a greater marvel to Rivers each day. He constantly searched them as one might study the crooks and turns of a new trail. He thought, perhaps one day I can ride their high trails.

They watered the horses in the Arkansas about mid-afternoon. The river was flowing swift and cold. The snow of the mountains transformed the lazy ribbon of water snaking its way across the plains into a rushing torrent of cold and clear earth blood.

Following the directions given by Peters, they left the Arkansas and headed due south. The mountains gave them a perfect guide to follow. After four days of travel they came upon another stream, smaller than the Arkansas, that seemed to flow out of a break in the mountains. They figured it to be the Pergatoire and followed it east away from the mountains. Two days later they began to see cattle grazing along the grassland close to the river. A closer look revealed Mexican herders holding the cattle.

They rode up to the wary cowhands and asked for directions to the Broken Wheel ranch.

"You are on it, senior," one of the men said. "What business do you have?"

"I am delivering horses to a Wilson Fennel. He bought them from our boss in Arkansas," Rivers replied.

"You are going in the right direction. Follow the river and you will see the ranch buildings up on the hill away from the river. You are about two hours away."

"Thanks," Rivers said as they rode away. He had noticed the cattle and they were in good shape. There was plenty of grass. He also took note of the ten or so men who were scattered around the cattle. The thought occurred to him that raising cattle around here required enough men to keep the Indians away.

They came up to the Broken Wheel from the river. Four riders met them a short distance from the river and inquired about their presence. Once again Rivers explained and they were directed to the gathering of buildings up ahead. One of the riders accompanied them and led them to the main ranch house. He dismounted and went into the house, returning immediately with a handsome gent the cowhand introduced as Wilson Fennel.

"Mr. Fennel, my name is Rivers." He nodded in the direction of his partners. "These men are Durham, Goldy, and Night Hawk. We're delivering the horses you bought from Mr. Peters back in Arkansas," Rivers said. "He said for me to give you this." Rivers handed over a letter to Fennel.

"Climb down and have a seat," Fennel said as he took the letter and walked to one of a number of chairs on the porch. He opened the letter and read it quickly. "So you are now the owner of the Crooked Wind."

"Yes. I didn't know Mr. Peters put that in his letter," Rivers said.

"He did and it is quite obvious he thinks a lot of you. He asked me to help you any way I can. He indicated you might have other business out this way," Fennel said.

"I do, but I would like to talk with you about that later. It's been a long ride and we have been away from good food and a bed for a spell. We've taken good care of your horses and we would be obliged if you would give us a place to sleep and rest up. When we've done that, I'd sure like to talk with you about a plan I have," Rivers said.

Fennel walked with them to look at the horses and it was obvious he was pleased. He told a couple of his men to take them to a corral and told another to show Rivers and his men where they could bunk.

"Supper will be ready in a couple of hours and you men are welcome to stay as long as you wish. If you stay too long, I'll put you to herding cattle," he said with a laugh.

They led their horses to a corral, stripped them, and followed the man to a bunkhouse close by. For the first time in a long time they were walking and talking without looking over their shoulder.

20

A night's sleep and two good home cooked meals were a welcomed change for Rivers and his men. It was obvious the Broken Wheel was a well run ranch. They had counted over forty hands around the ranch during supper and breakfast. Others were out on the range with the cattle. This was the largest operation any of them had ever been around. Most of the hands were Mexican. A few gringos were scattered here and there. It was amazing Fennel had built such a spread in this part of the country. Rivers was to meet with Fennel at his house at mid-morning and made his way to the well built Spanish style building.

Fennel was waiting for him on the porch and Rivers shook his hand and took a chair.

"Tell me about your plans," Fennel said.

"The reason I wanted to talk to you privately is because I have not shared them with my men. I'll do that when the time is right," Rivers said.

"I understand," Fennel replied.

"I bought the Crooked Wind from Mr. Peters to begin a two stage operation primarily focused on raising horses. Mr. Peters told me this part of the country was opening up to more trade and migration from back east. I feel like there is a future in the horse market out here. I brought your horses personally for two reasons. Mr. Peters described the horse you were riding as a McCloud horse. I have heard of McCloud horses since my days back in Georgia. Peters told me McCloud's ranch was somewhere out here and selfishly I wanted to visit it and get a close up of how he runs his business. My other reason for coming was to see if I could find some land suitable for a ranch and buy it," Rivers said.

"Peters was right about this area being more open to trade and migration. When the Mexicans sent the Spanish packing a lot changed about how the territory relates to the states back east. In fact, wagon trains are becoming commonplace with people bringing their wares this way from the east and Mexicans taking their trade items back that way. I got my land through a grant from the Spanish through a well placed official when I lived in Texas. McCloud got his the same way. In fact, any gringo land owners you find out here got theirs the same way. The Mexicans have really been easier to deal with than the Spanish. Most of my hands are Mexican and I have a good relationship with the government officials. I market my cattle through them. Up until the Mexicans took over, any trade taking place had to come through the Spanish hierarchy in Mexico," Fennel added.

"Tell me about the McCloud ranch. How far is it from here and would it be worth my time to visit it?"

"You can get there in about a week from here and it would be worthwhile for anybody interested in raising horses to visit it."

"Would he be willing to allow a stranger to look over his operation?"

"That's another matter. I've had dealings with McCloud and he seems to be a decent fellow. He has twin sons who give everybody fits. I don't know what you might run into if you told them you were thinking about starting a horse operation around these parts," Fennel said.

The thought of McCloud having two sons grabbed Rivers in the guts but he didn't let it show.

"Do you know of any land for sale or is it even possible for a person like me to buy land under the Mexican laws?"

"It's strange you asking that, especially with your interest in the McCloud ranching operation. There's a man named Roscoe Ames who owns land bordering McCloud's ranch. His ranch is the Circle Three. He got his land grant from the Spanish before me or McCloud. The Kiowas killed his son last year and he and his wife have had enough of fighting Indians while trying to raise cattle. I stop by his place every time I go down shopping for horses and the last time I was there he offered to sell me his land. McCloud wants it bad but he's determined not to sell to him. There's some bad blood between them. I think it has more to do with McCloud's boys than anything else. He may have sold it by now. I haven't heard if he has, but that wouldn't be unusual. I've had no reason to find out," Fennel said.

"Maybe I can find him and check on it," Rivers said.

"If you were going to be here a spell, I could find out for you. I'm scheduled to pick up a stallion from the McCloud ranch next week. I'd be glad to drop by his place and find out," Fennel said.

Rivers thought for a moment. "Mr. Fennel, I've had some fine mares belonging to you in my care for about six weeks. Would you trust me to bring your stallion back from the McCloud place?" Rivers asked.

"What you got on your mind?" Fennel asked.

"It would give me the very opportunity I need to look over the McCloud place and find out about the Circle Three at the same time. I'd be happy to take my men and go bring your horse back," Rivers said.

"I think we could work that out. It would spare me the men and time it would take and it would allow you to accomplish what you want. I don't mean to pry, but you don't seem like the kind of person who has the money to buy another ranch. Matter of fact, you don't seem like a person who had the money to buy the Crooked Wind. Do you have that kind of money?"

"I have the money," Rivers answered. "I would appreciate it if you allowed me to pick up your horse and escort him back."

Fennel smiled and revealed a look that told he was learning respect for the man sitting on his porch.

"Speaking of horses, you wouldn't want to sell that stallion you're riding?"

"You're not the only person who has shown interest in my horse. He's not for sale. Matter of fact, he will be the reason I'll one day have a horse ranch producing horses second to none, including McCloud," Rivers said.

Fennel laughed and said, "I can't argue with you there. He's the finest animal I believe I've ever seen."

"Tell me how I get to the Circle Three and McCloud's place."

"You go south along the mountains until you hit the Canadian river. She runs out of the mountains and alongside them until you are past McCloud's ranch. The Circle Three is right where the Mora river runs into the Canadian. The Circle Three lies east of the Canadian and runs along the river for about five miles. Most of Ames land is back up on the plains. McCloud's ranch borders the south boundary of the Circle Three. You'll be in the Colorado territory when you get to the Canadian. There are plenty of Indians and Mexican bandits for you to worry about so you'll have to be careful," Fennel said.

"We'll be all right. You write me a letter to give to McCloud and you can trust me with the money if I need to take it too," Rivers said.

"I'll get the letter ready. I've already paid for the horse. When do you plan to leave?"

"We'll rest here a couple more days and then head out if it's okay with you," Rivers said.

"That's fine. Proud to have you stay a while. Wouldn't mind if you turned that stallion in with a few of my mares while you're here," Fennel chuckled.

"That'll cost you and I haven't worked out the price yet," Rivers responded with a laugh.

"I'd appreciate it if you kept our arrangement between just the two of us."

"That's fine with me. Enjoy yourself while you are on the Broken Wheel."

They shook hands and Rivers walked back to where his pals were resting in the shade of one of the ranch buildings.

21

Rivers rode off the Broken Wheel five days later. He was in the company of his good friends and beautiful country. He told the boys they were going to a horse ranch owned by a man named Matthew McCloud. They would be bringing back a stallion for Mr. Fennel and use the trip as an opportunity to view a first class horse raising operation.

The trail was easy for the first day and they came up to the Canadian river late on the second day. They crossed it in some shallows and rode west. The land on the east was too difficult for riding close to the river.

Rivers spent a lot of time thinking about Matthew McCloud. He wondered what it would be like when he saw him for the first time. A part of him wanted to walk right up and say I'm your son. I was born to the woman you broke your promise to back in Georgia. Another part of him wanted to kill him or make him hurt like his mother. Then there was a part he fought against. He couldn't push aside the thought of what his real father might be like. Red Wolf was the closest thing to a father in his life. Maybe it would have been different for his mother and him if his father had returned for her. But he didn't come back. The battle inside was caused by his mother's words. She had stressed that Rivers would like him when he found him. No. I won't, Rivers thought.

Rivers and his friends worked easily together on the trail. The journey from Fort Smith to the Broken Wheel forged a sense of interdependence between them. They all knew what to do and how to do it. When it came to making camp, cooking, standing watch, or careful riding during the day, each man knew his back would always be covered and he would personally stand for the other three. Rivers and Goldy were a lot alike. Both were quiet and moved with ease in accomplishing any task. Durham, much more subdued than when Rivers first encountered him, was the jokester and life of the four. Night Hawk was perhaps the most respected of the group. He did his work without fanfare and brought a dimension to their life on the trail because of his knowledge of this part of the country.

Their travel was without incident and they came to the Mora river on the fourth day. They crossed the Canadian at the mouth of the Mora and immediately began to see cattle wearing the Circle Three brand.

"Is this the ranch?" Goldy asked.

"No," Rivers replied. "I do want to meet the man who owns it though."

They followed the river and came up to some wranglers watching the cattle. They rode up to them.

"Howdy," Rivers said. "Is Roscoe Ames around? If he is, I'd sure like to talk to him."

"Si Senor," the Mexican wrangler said. "Follow the river and you will see the ranch about a mile down that way."

As they rode away, Goldy asked with a puzzled look, "Who is Roscoe Ames and how'd you know to ask about him?"

"Mr. Fennel told me about him. I hear he might be interested in selling his ranch and I want to talk to him about it," Rivers said.

"You thinking about buying it?" Goldy asked with the puzzle becoming a little more difficult.

"Yep," Rivers answered and rode on ahead.

They came to the ranch setting back on the high ground from the river. As they rode up, they were met by two wranglers.

"My name is Rivers and I'd like to talk with Roscoe Ames," Rivers said. "Is he around?"

"He's right here," a voice spoke from the porch. "Step down and talk." A short stocky man stepped down from the porch and extended his hand to Rivers. "I'm Roscoe Ames. What can I do for you?"

"I'm Rivers." He motioned to the others in succession and said, "This is Goldy, Durham, and Night Hawk. They ride for me off the Crooked Wind ranch back in Arkansas. We delivered some horses to Mr. Fennel up at the Broken Wheel and are on our way to pick up a horse for him at the McCloud operation."

"Good to meet you," Ames said. "Always glad to have company. You said you wanted to talk to me but I don't have nothing to do with McCloud's ranch. You're still a half days ride before you get to his ranch."

"Why I'm here is Mr. Fennel told me you might be interested in selling your ranch," Rivers said.

"I am if I can find a buyer. There's not a lot of folks with the money and determination to fight the Indians to stay here. The Kiowa got my son over a year ago. Killed him and two of my hands. His mother has give up on this place and I guess I have to. McCloud wants to buy the place bad and he's offered me more than it's worth," Ames said.

"Then why haven't you sold it to him?" Rivers asked.

"Because I don't cotton to the way he does things. Well, maybe not him. It's his boys. I reckon McCloud ain't that bad. His boys are another matter. They like to ride high in the saddle and look down on everybody else. I ain't much, but I ain't never crawled on my belly for no man and I sure ain't gonna do it for them two," Ames said.

"What did they do to rile you?" Goldy asked. He was getting interested now and there was something about Ames he liked.

"I've had two or three run ins with em. The last one was when they drove some of their cattle across my place and scattered my herd all to hell. When I rode out to complain about it them two boys tried to goad me into a shooting fight. I ain't much with that sort of thing and backed down. They told me to start shooting or shut up. Ever since that day I made up my mind it'll snow in the summer before I sell to em."

"Did their father know what they did?" Rivers asked.

"Don't know. He don't hardly get out any more. He hangs close to the ranch and lets them boys run things. He did come over here and try to buy the place. Had them boys with him. When I turned down his offer, he was nice enough and thanked me before he rode off. One of his boys hung back and told me I'd sell to them or I wouldn't sell at all. I've had a few people interested in the place but nothing ever comes of it. I think McCloud is getting to em and scaring em off."

"Would you sell me the ranch?" Rivers asked.

"If you've got the money, I'll flat sell it to you," Ames said.

"The money is not a problem," Rivers said. "Would it be possible for us to stay the night here and look the place over tomorrow? After I have seen it, we can talk about your asking price and do a little dealing."

"The boys will show you a place to sleep and we'll have supper in a little while. Ya'll make yourselves at home," Ames said.

They followed a couple of cowhands to a bunkhouse and unloaded their gear. They were alone when Rivers began to explain to his friends.

"I'm going to buy this place and we are going to go into the horse business out here," Rivers said. "I know you fellows are a little shocked at all this, but it has been my plan all along."

"I ain't surprised at much you do," Goldy said. "I just can't get used to riding with a ugly cowhand who has the kind of money to go around buying ranches. Are you sure you got that much money?"

"Yep," Rivers said and smiled.

Goldy smiled back and said, "I ain't asking where you got it."

"And I ain't telling," Rivers replied.

They settled in, ate a good supper with Ames and his men, and bedded down for a good night's sleep.

Rivers and Ames rode out the next morning so Rivers could get a good look at what he was planning to buy. The land along the Canadian was good grazing. There were about three hundred acres of grazing near the ranch house.

"This is good grazing for most of the year," Ames said. "Only three times since I've been here has the river got up so high I had to move the stock off. This is where I bring my cattle when I need them in close."

"It looks good," Rivers replied. "What about the grass on the rest of your land?"

"We will go up high and I'll show you. There's plenty for the stock I run and then some," Ames said.

The land shot up about a hundred feet at the edge of the grassland and then rose gradually for another hundred. The climb was carefully chosen by Ames and they reached the top to look back down on the ranch. It was a beautiful sight. They then rode for about three hours with Ames pointing out landmarks he used to identify his property lines. The land up high opened onto a flat plain holding trees and scrub brush separated by areas of plentiful prairie grass. The cattle had kept the area clean.

When they came down off the high ground they followed a well used trail about twenty feet wide. It was obvious from the tracks Ames used this trail to move his cattle up and down. A walk over the area around the ranch house led them through three barns, two bunk houses, a tour of the corrals and tack building.

They walked back to the ranch house and took a seat on the porch to talk business.

"How much are you asking?" Rivers asked.

"I've give it a lot of thought. I've got about four thousand acres, give or take a little. It's good grazing with plenty of water. I've got four hundred brood cows and some good bulls. The house, buildings, and tack are all in good shape. It's worth more than I'm asking, cause there ain't a lot of buyers around and the man who would pay me more than it's worth ain't gonna get it. I'll have to get seven thousand dollars for the whole thing. I know that's probably a lot of money for you, but it will have to take care of me when I get back east."

"Sounds like a fair price to me. It's plain to see the place is in good shape and it's exactly what I'm looking for. I'll take your offer," Reed answered.

"You got that kind of money?" Ames asked.

"Yes I do. How soon do you want to get out of here?"

"As soon as I can."

"Where's the nearest town with a bank?" Rivers asked.

"That'd be Santa Rosa. Don't take me wrong, but I ain't leaving here with Mexican money. I'm afraid you might have a hard time with the bank," Ames said.

"The bank is not necessary. Will you take gold?"

"Be glad to," Ames said with a chuckle.

"Well, I've got to get Mr. Fennell's horse back to him. Then I can come back and bring you the money and we can take care of getting the deed signed. It will probably be two to three weeks before I get back. Will that be all right?"

"That'll be fine. You'll need some hands. I've got eight and they are the best you can find anywhere. Five of them are tough as nails Mexicans. The other three are strong men too. They are loyal and good workers. All are good with cattle. I'd appreciate it if you could keep them on. They need the work and you couldn't find any better. Pablo, one of the Mexicans, lives in the small house over yonder and his wife, Maria, cooks for us. You can't beat her cooking."

"It would be a big help to me if they can stay on," Rivers said.

Ames gave Rivers a serious look for a moment and asked, "This is for real ain't it?"

Rivers smiled and pulled some coins out of his pocket. He handed them to Ames and said, "Here's three hundred dollars. If I don't come back, you can keep it."

Ames rolled the gold coins in his hand for a minute and then handed them back. "Nope. I'm a man of my word and that's how I do business. Your word is good enough for me."

"Then we've got a deal. If you don't mind, we will stay the night here and go on to McCloud's ranch in the morning. That will give me a chance to meet your hands and tell them a little about my plans for the place."

"I don't mind. We'll be glad to have you," Ames said.

Rivers walked back to the corral where Durham, Goldy, and Night Hawk were resting. "Well men, we now own this ranch. Sort of. I haven't paid him yet but I will as soon as we can get Fennell's horse home and get back here."

The three friends looked at Rivers with a shocked look and as usual, it was Goldy who spoke. "Rivers, I figure I'm learning there's a lot more to you than most folks know. Forgive me for looking like the last kid out for recess. I ain't never rode with no cowhand that could spend the kind of money you're throwing around." He looked at his buddy and asked, "Have you really got that much?"

"It's a long story Goldy. I may never tell it. It's real personal. I've got that much and I didn't steal it, if you are thinking that."

"No. I ain't thought no such thing. You don't have to tell me neither. It's your business."

"Men, I'm going to build the best horse ranch in the west. I'd like for you all to be here with me. Goldy, you'll be my foreman. It would make me proud if you will help me."

They looked at each other for a brief spell and all three said they would work for him.

"Here's my plan," Rivers said. "Me and Goldy will go on the McCloud ranch tomorrow morning. Night Hawk, I want you and Durham to head out from here and get back to the Crooked Wind as fast as you can. I hope my young mares will be there from Georgia. If they are not, then wait on them. As soon as they arrive, head back here. I want you to bring Mary with you. You know how much I trust you to ask you to get my sister out here safely."

"You won't have to worry about your sister," Durham said. "Ain't nothing gonna happen to her with me around."

Night Hawk added, "We will be worthy of your trust Rivers."

"I know it. Me and Goldy will get back here and get this place ready for winter. By the time spring comes I'll start looking for you. I'm going to keep the hands Mr. Ames has working for him. We'll meet them tonight. This is a long time dream of mine and you don't know how it makes me feel to have you a part of it. Durham, I'll talk to Mr. Ames about any provisions you will need to get started and you can pack them on one of the packhorses tonight. I'll be fine when you and Mary are here."

After supper, with all the men on the ranch present, Ames called them out onto the porch. "Men, I want you to meet the man you'll be working for before long," he said. "His name is Rivers. I'm selling him the ranch and he wants you to stay on."

"That's right. I sure do. I'll need your help and Mr. Ames tells me you are good men. I promise to work you hard, pay you a fair wage, and stand with you in any trouble we face. I'll work as hard as you do and won't ask you to do anything I won't tangle with myself."

"Sounds good to me Mr. Rivers," a slender cowhand said. "I'm Zeke Perkins."

"Good to meet you Zeke. How about the rest of you?"

"I'm Pablo Mesa. These men are Rafael Furcales, Mule Martinez, Raul Santos, and Filipe Estabal. We have worked for Mr. Ames for five years and we think we have done a good job. We will work hard for you," Mesa continued.

"Good. I understand your wife cooks for the ranch Pablo. Do you speak for her too?"

"I do senor."

"I promise you your wife will be treated with respect in my house."

Rivers then looked at the other two men. "What about you?"

"My name's Bolton. Clyde Bolton. Most folks call me Slick. This here's Nub Foster. Nub's too lazy to travel so I'll guess he'll stay. He'd lay down and die if I didn't kick him in the rear every now and then. I guess I'll stay just to keep him alive," Bolton said with a horse laugh. "To tell you the truth, me and Nub, along with Zeke and these greazers will work hard for you and ride for the brand."

Pablo smiled and said, "He's going to call me a greazer some day and I'm going to slit his throat."

It was obvious to Rivers the men got along well with each other.

"I want you men to meet Goldy Freeman. He'll be your foreman. This is Night Hawk, Kiowa warrior and close friend," Rivers said as he pointed to his breed pal. "This is Roscoe Durham. He'll be the last one standing when the fight is over. You'll be proud to have him on your side." Rivers motioned toward Durham and the big man swelled with pride.

"We're going to raise horses. We'll keep enough cattle to keep the range grazed until we get the horse operation up and running and then we will cut back on them. We will always have some cattle on the place. Can you handle the change?" Rivers asked.

They all agreed and seemed excited about it. They talked among themselves for a spell and Rivers shared with them his dream. When the talking was done, they went to the bunkhouse to settle in for the night. Tomorrow would bring a new challenge for Rivers and his friends.

22

Rivers saw Night Hawk and Durham off the next morning, bid farewell to Mr. Ames, and he and Goldy headed south toward the Bar M. Ames told them they would be on Bar M land soon after leaving and sure enough cattle wearing the Bar M brand started showing up within an hour. They saw no outriders and it was getting on to noon when they spotted a large group of buildings they figured to be the ranch. They drew closer and were met by two wranglers who rode out to inquire about the reason for their presence.

"We've come to pick up a stallion for Mr. Fennel up in Colorado," Goldy said.

"Follow us on up to the house and we'll tell the boss and sort him out for you," one of the riders said.

They followed the men and were a little bug-eyed at the size of the operation. There were at least five good sized barns and numerous corrals. It looked like they had three large bunk houses. The main house was bigger than anything the two men had ever seen. It sat in the middle of some giant cottonwoods. The place was crawling with men. At a glance Rivers counted upwards of twenty-five busy here and there.

The corrals were crowded with the most beautiful gather of horseflesh Rivers had ever seen. It made Mr. Griggs' operation back in Georgia look small.

The men leading them pulled up in front of one of the barns and tied their horses. Rivers and Goldy followed suit. Some of the men quit what they were doing and walked around Rivers' horse admiring the black stallion.

"That's some horse you're riding feller," one of them said. "Where'd you get him?"

"Back east," Rivers said, not wanting to talk too much.

One of the men who led them up to the house walked around the crowd to a big fellow who was also caught up in admiring Rivers' horse. "These gents came to get a stallion for a man named Fennel up in Colorado," he said.

The big man walked around to them and said, "I'm Bob Cutler, foreman of the Bar M. We've been looking for you to show up. We've got your horse over in the barn."

Rivers breathed a sigh of relief. He had thought the big man could possibly have been Matthew McCloud. Before he could respond to Cutler, two young men rode up and dismounted. They looked to be twins. They walked cockily into the group of men and measured the awesome features of the big stallion.

"Where'd he come from?" one of the twins asked Cutler.

"Belongs to this man," Cutler said, pointing toward Rivers. "They're here to pick up the Fennel horse."

"What'll you take for the stallion?" the other twin asked.

"He's not for sale," Rivers answered.

The two brothers took in the tall dark skinned cowboy who stood a good six inches taller than them.

"Come on now. Everything's for sale at some price. What'll it take?" the first asked.

"It will take a lot more than you've got," Rivers said with a casual assurance.

It was apparent both young men were accustomed to getting what they wanted. Rivers had already tagged them as the McCloud boys before Cutler introduced them.

"Fellers, this here is Toby McCloud and this is his brother Tyler. I didn't get your names," Cutler said.

"Mine is Rivers and my partner's name is Goldy," Rivers said.

"Rivers is it," Toby said. "Well, Rivers, I'd sure like to tell you how much money we got. I'd bet we could buy this horse."

"You'd lose," Rivers responded.

Cutler was enjoying how the stranger was handling the twins, but he sensed the boys were getting a little agitated and he changed the subject. "Do you plan on heading right back to Colorado?"

"Yes. We want to make the trip as soon as possible," Goldy said.

"Well, we'll run him out and get him ready for you," Cutler said.

"Sure," Rivers said. "I'll need to see a Matthew McCloud. He told me to give him this letter personally."

"That won't be necessary," Tyler McCloud said. "I'll give it to him."

"It will be necessary. I work for a man who trusted me to do a job. I'll do the job he told me to do," Rivers said.

Both McCloud boys stood with faces growing red. They couldn't believe this cowhand was talking to them like they were nobody. Cutler headed it off with a smile.

"Come on with me," he said. "I'll take you up to meet Mr. McCloud."

"Wait a minute Cutler," Toby said.

""No, you wait a minute," Cutler responded. "According to your father's orders, I'm the foreman of this ranch. I don't listen to nobody but him. When he tells me different, I'll do it different. If you got a problem with that, you talk to him. Now, if you men will follow me."

They walked off leaving the McCloud boys twitching in their tracks. Rivers smiled at them as he turned to follow Cutler.

Rivers breathed deeply as he walked toward the house. His emotions were in every direction. How does a twenty year old man see his father for the first time. The man does not know I exist, he thought. The brief walk allowed Rivers to calm down a bit. He couldn't help but reflect upon the kind of boys Matthew McCloud had raised. They both must have taken after their mother. His mother had said Matthew McCloud was a big man. The brothers were short and a bit on the light side.

Cutler stopped at the porch and asked a servant to take a message to Mr. McCloud. "Tell him I have a little business for him."

Momentarily the door swung open and a big man filled the opening. Rivers looked up to see a man who weighed every bit of two hundred sixty pounds. He had brown curly locks spilling down to his ears. He was wide at the shoulders with big hands attached to long arms hanging well below his waist.

"Morning Bob. What you got so important you'd take me away from my coffee?" the big man asked as he stepped off the porch and faced Cutler and the two strangers.

Rivers sized him up. They were about the same height. The big man had come off the porch with ease of movement. He stood relaxed and smiling before them.

"Boss, these men came down from Colorado to get the horse you're holding for Fennel. Introduce yourselves to Matthew McCloud, boys," Cutler said.

Rivers remained silent. His eyes met McClouds. Rivers eyes were searching. McCloud sensed something and broke the silence.

"Matt McCloud," he said as he extended his hand.

"My name's Rivers," he said as he extended his hand as well.

The two big men stood, hands clasped, for an unusual length of time. Strength to strength, it was as if the young man was measuring the older. McCloud held his position, looking into the eyes of the stranger. There was something about the eyes. What was it? Had he met this man before? A brief chill ran down the back of a strong man who did not experience such emotions often.

McCloud released the grip and extended his hand to Goldy.

"Freeman's the name Mr. McCloud," Goldy said.

"Good to meet you men. We've been expecting somebody to come get the horse. We've got him ready. Why did you need to see me?"

"Mr. Peters told me to give this letter to you personally," Rivers said as he pulled a leather pouch from his pocket.

"Well, you've done your job," McCloud said as he took the pouch without opening it. "Tell him I hope he enjoys the horse. Be careful on your way back."

"Thank you. We will," Rivers said as he turned and walked away. Goldy followed.

McCloud watched them. There was something about the man named Rivers he couldn't figure out.

"Strange man," McCloud said to Cutler as he motioned toward Rivers. "Did you see how he looked at me? For a minute there I felt like somebody was walking on my grave."

"I got a feeling he's a tough man. Stood up to your boys like they was flies buzzing around his head," Cutler said smiling.

"You mean Toby and Tyler cornered him?"

"Tried to. He's riding the best looking stallion I've ever seen. No offense boss. You don't have nothing on the place that would measure up to his horse. Your boys pushed him to sell it and he didn't budge. The thing is, he didn't even seem nervous around them two. Don't nobody know what they might do."

"Let's go see the horse," McCloud said as he walked toward the barn. They came up to the two men as they were preparing to lead the new horse out to their mounts.

'My, my," McCloud said. "That's some more horse." He walked slowly around Rivers horse, taking in the long legs and strong body unlike anything he had ever seen, and he had seen plenty.

When Rivers and Goldy led the new horse out, McCloud was standing there in amazement.

"Rivers, I don't mean to pry. I sure would like to know where you got him," McCloud said, lifting his hand toward the big stallion.

"I got him back east when he was a colt. Raised him. He's something else ain't he?"

"He's got some bloodlines in him from fine horses. Where'd you get him?"

Rivers watched the big man's eyes for a reaction. "Man I got him from said he was a Griggs horse. I don't know what that means," Rivers said.

McCloud's eyes lit up. "I know what it means. There's a man in

Georgia named Griggs who raises the best horses in them parts. My father used to do some business with him."

"You from Georgia?" Rivers asked.

"Lived there for a while. Came out here with my family. Matter of fact, we brought along a few of Griggs mares when we left there. That's some coincidence. You wouldn't want to sell your horse would you?"

"No. He's not for sale," Rivers replied.

"I can understand that. If you ever do decide to sell him, look me up," McCloud said.

"That won't ever happen. He's like family," Rivers said.

"Ya'll be careful," the big man said as he turned and walked back toward the house. Rivers thanked Cutler for his help and they headed out toward Colorado.

They were about an hour away from the Bar M when they topped a small knoll and found the McCloud twins in front of them, obviously waiting for them.

"Let me handle this," Rivers said to Goldy as they drew nearer. Both men were riding with their rifles across their saddles and they casually moved them to point generally toward the two waiting men.

"You waiting for us?" Rivers asked.

"Thought we might clear up a thing or two with you," Toby said.

"Clear away," Rivers shot back.

"Don't ever set foot on the Bar M again," Tyler said. "If you do, you won't be riding off." He had a quirky smile shadowing his tough words.

"We mean it," Toby added. "You sounded kinda smart back there. I was wondering if you feel the same way now?"

"Let me tell you how I'm feeling right now," Rivers answered. "I'm feeling like dragging you off your horses and slapping some sense into your head. I've got a stronger feeling of blowing a hole clean through you. Both would be real easy to do. Believe me, they would. The only way you can keep it from happening is to be grave yard quiet and ride away without looking back. You say a word and you're mine. I'm counting to ten in my head. When I get there, you don't get to choose." Rivers was as calm as a baby calf lying in the sunshine. Goldy was on edge and ready.

The McCloud boys wanted to say something. It was not working out like they figured. They just wanted to put the two cowhands in their place and send them off with a little fear. But these men were not afraid. They looked at each other and simultaneously pulled their horses around and rode toward the ranch house.

Rivers and Goldy watched them until they were out of sight.

"Thought sure we was going to have a shooting," Goldy said.

"I didn't. You see their eyes? Both of them got eyes ain't never still. Bouncing all the time. Kind of shooting they'll do is when your back is turned. Now their daddy, he'd shoot you straight up. He'll look you right in the eye," Rivers said.

"All the same, we ain't seen the last of them two. When we get back here and start ranching, we'll have to deal with them," Goldy warned.

Rivers laughed. "We'll spank'em too." They rode on toward Colorado.

23

Three months later.

The move to the Circle Three went smoothly for Rivers and Goldy. Upon arrival they jumped into the work and were well on the way to transforming the place into a horse ranch.

A new corral for horses was complete. It included three catch pens adjacent to it and one breeding pen. One of the two barns was reworked to provide ten stalls to use when foaling time came.

Rivers worked daily with two things occupying his mind. He constantly thought about his sister and her safety on the journey out. He knew Night Owl and Durham would do their best to take care of her. The worry came from the long trip through tough country and the countless ruffians and hostile Indians between him and Arkansas.

The other thing was not a thing. It was Matthew McCloud. It felt strange being so close to his father. Knowing what he looked like and where he was did not calm the feelings he had for the man. The day would come when he would confront McCloud and tell him how low-down he was. For now it could wait. He wanted to get his horse operation up and running. He had not seen McCloud or any of his hands since moving onto the ranch. He assumed they had no idea he now owned the place. It would suit him fine to keep it like that.

Two days back something happened causing Rivers to add to his thinking list. He had been coming back from checking the cattle up on top and spotted movement ahead of him. He was well back in some scrub and stopped to check it out. A hunting party of Kiowa was moving east across his place. There were six Indians and they were leading three horses laden with elk meat. He watched them until they moved out of sight.

He had learned from the hands on the ranch that the Kiowa tribe was responsible for most of the Indian conflict on the ranch and they camped in their primary village due east. They usually traveled across the ranch when going to the mountains for hunting. They also killed and butchered cattle throughout the year. He had been told any cattle left unattended was wide open for them.

Rivers planned to go out and have a heart to heart talk with their chief. He did not want to spend his time killing his blood brothers. On the other hand, he did not plan to live at their mercy.

24

The wind coming down the river had a fresh chill to it when Rivers walked outside the next morning. He knew it would not be long before the weather would begin to change. He called Goldy over and told him of his plans to visit the Kiowa village.

"You've got to let me go with you," Goldy said.

"No. I need you here. I'll be gone a couple of days. Three at the most. You take care of things here and don't worry about me. I'll be fine," Rivers said.

Rivers put a few things together and shook hands with his partner before leaving. He rode up to the high ground and headed due east. A couple of hours away from the ranch he pulled up in a stand of thick scrub brush. It lay just below the crest of the last prominent high ground looking out on a broken plain of rolling prairie. He stripped the saddle from his horse and stashed it in the brush. He took off his shirt and boots. He was wearing some old buckskin pants. He donned his moccasins. Leaving his hat, boots, and rifle by his saddle, he swung up on his horse and settled in on the saddle blanket he had left there. He then rode out of the brush and over the high ground.

The Kiowa, from all indications, made their home on the plains. It was his desire to meet them and talk. He knew well the danger of his actions. He also knew he needed to have an understanding with them if he was to make it ranching. He couldn't spend all his time protecting his cattle or horses.

He was told the Kiowa had their village along a small creek running north to south across the plain. He rode east to find the creek and then he would look for their village. He kept his eyes open for sign and saw a lot of tracks left by unshod horses. He ran across some fresh prints heading in the direction he was going so he followed them. About an hour later he saw a bit of dust rising from the trail up ahead.

Relaxed, he rode on ready for whatever came his way. His only visible weapon was his knife. His primary weapon was his knowledge of Indians and his proficiency in dealing with them. Night Hawk had given him a good usage of their language. He hoped he could get close enough to use it.

When he approached the place where he had seen the dust, he saw where the tracks led up a small draw. He assumed they had spotted him on their back trail and had planned a welcome for him.

He rode into the draw completely aware he could receive an arrow in the back at any moment. Instead, he rounded a curve to find himself between two young Kiowa warriors. They were on opposite sides of the trail. Their horses were elevated a little higher than his and both men had their bows rigged for action. Rivers pulled his horse to a stop and looked straight ahead, purposely keeping his eyes off the warriors.

"It is a good day for the Kiowa," Rivers spoke in their dialect. "I am Rivers, Cherokee warrior from the high mountains of the big waters where the sun appears. I would speak to your chief. Take me to him."

"You speak our tongue," one of the warriors replied.

"Speaking your tongue is not hard to do," Rivers said. He changed and spoke in Cherokee, "Do you speak mine?"

The two men did not understand his last statement and looked dumbfounded.

"Why do you wish to speak with Big Elk?" one asked.

"I will tell him my reasons. I do not waste my time with little warriors who hunt rabbits," Rivers said.

Both men grunted their distaste for his insolence.

"Hunting rabbits, you think," the first warrior to speak shot back. "We have you beneath the power of two arrows and you call us rabbit hunters.

You must be the rabbit." Both warriors laughed.

"You have me nowhere," Rivers said. "I rode in here knowing of your presence and your snare. If I feared you, you both would be dead now and your scalps hanging on my horse. If I must kill you, then I will. I prefer to speak with your chief."

"Kill us. How would you kill us, rabbit in the snare? Why do you not look at us? Are you afraid?" one asked. They both laughed.

Rivers turned to look deep into the eyes of the last warrior to speak. He then shifted his eyes to the other and looked into his soul. Letting the effect of his confident gaze sink in, Rivers finally spoke. "Tell me little boys, do you see fear in my eyes? I will ask you one last time to take me to your chief. I will talk with you no longer. You can lead the way or get ready to die."

The Kiowa warriors looked to each other for direction and neither had it to offer. Could this strange man kill them? The air was tense and both felt their nerves twitch, but the strange man sat his horse as if nothing bothered him.

Finally one warrior spoke. "Follow us and we will take you to Big Elk."

Rivers breathed a hidden relief as he fell in behind one warrior and was followed by the other.

They rode a twisted trail east until they came up to a creek. It was running with water but nowhere was it over a foot deep. They crossed it and turned south. They rode for an hour before riding away from the creek. They climbed a gradual ascending trail that topped out overlooking a valley literally covered with lodges and Indians.

As they rode down toward the village other warriors rode out to encircle the trio. The new arrivals shot questioning glares at Rivers who effectively deflected them by riding very relaxed with his eyes straight ahead. He tried to sit as straight as possible on the big stallion to accent his size. The Kiowa were noticeably shorter in stature.

They rode into the village and suddenly the two warriors leading him pulled up and slid from their ponies. They motioned for him to do likewise.

He slid off his horse and dropped the reins to the ground.

"Wait here," one warrior said as he walked away.

A large crowd of Kiowa gathered around Rivers. Their primary interest was in his horse. He listened as they spoke of the big horse. All of them admired him. Not knowing he understood their tongue, one warrior suggested that perhaps Big Elk would allow them to compete for the horse instead of claiming it for himself.

"No Kiowa warrior or Big Elk will ride my horse," Rivers spoke in a firm but relaxed voice. "He belongs to this Cherokee warrior from the high mountains where the sun appears. No Kiowa warrior could ever take him."

They were astonished at his ability to speak their language. Before they could respond, the warrior returned to lead Rivers to Big Elk.

The other warrior who accompanied Rivers into the village looked at his brothers and broke into a big smile. "He calls us hunters of rabbits." They then laughed with him, admiring the courage of the lone warrior.

Rivers was ushered into a large lodge and knew immediately which of the five men sitting inside was Big Elk. The warrior leading him motioned for Rivers to sit and as he reclined, the warrior sat beside him.

No one moved or spoke. Rivers assumed a confident posture with his eyes fixing on no single person.

After a period of silence, the chief spoke. "I am Big Elk. Spotted Horse tells me you came upon our land wishing to speak with me."

"I came for that purpose. You are known as a great chief with much wisdom. My words are for you. I will not speak before the old men seated by you or this young hunter of rabbits," Rivers said, motioning toward the warrior called Spotted Horse.

The chief registered no emotion as he received the challenge to a private conversation. The silence was like a cyclone until Big Elk motioned for the others to leave."

When alone, Big Elk spoke. "Speak your words to me."

"I am Rivers of the Cherokee tribe. Our home is in the high mountains where the sun appears. The white man has forced my people from their homeland to a worthless land far away. I escaped and came into your land to make my place. I will run no more. I came here to live or die. I will not be a slave to the white man. They took our lands and our life. They do not know how to speak the truth.

"It is not of my doing, but I have white man's blood in me. I hate it. My word is true. I am not white. I am Indian. I am not afraid to die at the hands of the Kiowa. It would be an honor. I will not live or die by the hands of the white man.

"I brought with me the shining rocks I dug from my homeland. With these rocks I have bought the ranch where the two rivers join just below the high mountains. You know it well. Your warriors have raided there often for the white man's cattle.

"I came to offer you my hand of peace. I do not desire to kill my brothers, the Kiowa. If you take my hand of peace, you may cross my land at any time without fear. I know you go to the mountains to hunt. I will also allow you to take twenty of my cows during the cold winter when game is scarce. I will leave them on the high ground where you can get to them easily. You may take them only in the winter. In return, you will leave me and my ranch alone when you raid."

"And what if I refuse your hand of peace?" Big Elk asked.

"Then Kiowa will die. I have no doubt you can raid my ranch and take my cattle. I speak more words of truth. If you do, I will come after you and avenge my loss with Kiowa blood."

"You speak boldly for one who sits alone in the middle of my village," Big Elk said.

"Big Elk, I could kill you now before you could call for help. That is not why I came. I could have killed the child warriors who brought me here. I am not here as a prisoner. I am here to speak words of truth with a strong chief. If your answer to my hand of peace is no, then I fully expect to ride out of your village with the same respect I had for you when I came. If for some reason the people who told me of your greatness were wrong, then we will both just die here. I'm prepared to do that. It would honor me to die in battle with the great Big Elk," Rivers said.

"You are truly Indian, even though the white man's blood shows. I think it will be good to have you in our land. I will accept your hand of peace with one condition. We both will understand the boundary for your cattle and you must not cross into our land or hunt here," Big Elk responded.

"I agree. I am proud you are a wise chief. I wish to offer you a gift. When I leave, I ask you to look at my horse. There is no finer animal anywhere. I will raise horses on my ranch. I offer you the first male he sires as a gift. You can breed it with your horses and it will not be long until the Kiowa are known for their horses as well as their courage in battle," Rivers said.

"I would welcome such a gift. What would you ask of me?" Big Elk asked.

"You know the other Indian tribes that hunt or raid in this land. I would ask you to tell them all the Cherokee warrior who owns the ranch is your friend. Perhaps it would keep me from killing them. I can get more horses or cattle. That is not a problem. I have no desire to kill my brothers," Rivers said.

"I will do it," Big Elk responded.

Rivers and Big Elk stood. They clasped hands and looked deep into each other's eyes.

"Come with me," Big Elk said.

Rivers followed the chief out of the lodge and toward the gathering of Indians surrounding his horse. They parted to allow the two to walk up close to the horse.

"You spoke truth, Cherokee brother. The horse is above all I've seen." Big Elk walked around the big stallion, taking in every inch of the fine horse. He turned outward and spoke to his warriors. "Listen to me. I have declared a peace between the Kiowa and Rivers, the Cherokee warrior. His ranch along the Canadian will be for our use, but we will not take anything or harm anyone there. I have spoken. Hear me well."

A voice came from crowd. "He has called us weak and hunters of rabbits. Why make peace with one who has not shown us his strength?"

The crowd moved aside to reveal the speaker, a stocky warrior who appeared to be in his thirties.

"Do you question me Grey Fox?" Big Elk asked.

"I do not question our great warrior chief. I wish to show the rider of this horse I am more than a hunter of rabbits," Grey Fox answered.

Big Elk turned to Rivers. "Your words have insulted this strong warrior. Grey Fox has had many victories in battle. Will you turn from your calling the Kiowa hunters of rabbits?"

"I do not turn from my words. If Grey Fox desires to test my strength, let him do so," Rivers replied.

"Eee yi," Grey Fox yelled. "Choose your weapon."

"I only have my knife. I choose not to use it. I do not want to kill you," Rivers said.

Grey Fox laughed. "What makes you think you can kill me with the knife. I know how to fight with the knife."

Rivers backed away from the crowd a few steps and turned toward a woodpile near a fire. It was about twenty paces away. "Grey Fox, the top log on the pile wears your name. The knot near the center is your heart."

In one fluid motion, taking the warriors by surprise, Rivers drew the knife and threw it. The knife sank deep into the knot. A murmur broke through the warriors. Rivers walked to the pile and retrieved his knife. He slipped it back into the leather sheaf riding low on his right hip and turned to face the men.

"If you choose the knife, I will kill you. I would rather be a brother to the strong Kiowa warrior named Grey Fox. It is obvious he is not a hunter of rabbits."

Big Elk had a broad smile across his face. It was also obvious he had made peace with a strong Cherokee warrior.

Grey Fox swelled with pride because the rider of the big horse had recanted and recognized him as a warrior and not a hunter of rabbits.

"You have made peace with a strong man," Grey Fox said to Big Elk. "It is good we do not make war." The warrior stepped close to Rivers. "Would you let me hold your knife?"

Rivers pulled it slowly and flipped it deftly to present the handle to Grey Fox.

The warrior examined it carefully, admiring it's size and perfect balance. He ran his fingers along the sharp blade and then the rounded knob on the handle.

"Would you teach me to throw the knife as you do?" Grey Fox asked.

"I will do more. I will have you a knife made like mine. Then I will teach you to throw it." Rivers took the knife back and again turned to the wood pile. He threw the knife so the blunt knob at the handle's end hit the top log at the same knot. Rivers smiled for the first time since entering the village and spoke in a low voice, as if embarrassed, "I use that end when I hunt rabbits."

All the warriors laughed. A brotherhood was established in this moment. It would serve Rivers and the Kiowa well for a long time.

25

Rivers returned to the ranch and told Goldy and the men about his visit with the Kiowa and the peace he made with them.

"When you see them on our place, keep your distance and allow them safe travel. We will place cattle for them to take during winter in a spot I'll point out later. If you encounter any hostility from them, back off and come tell me. I will keep my word with them," Rivers said.

The men understood and agreed. To a man they had no problem with leaving the Kiowa alone.

The next four months were busy. The cattle were brought low along the river and fared well on the grass that remained and the hay laid up for them. The men used the time to brand all the stock with the Crooked Wind brand, the new name of the ranch. As the weather changed, Rivers got the itch to see his sister. He hoped everything was going well for Durham and Nighthawk. He would just feel better when they returned.

He had seen Matthew McCloud only once since buying the ranch. A couple of weeks after Mr. Ames left the ranch McCloud and his foreman rode into the ranch yard. Rivers went out to meet them. There were no pleasantries between the two and that suited Rivers perfectly.

"Some of my hands saw Roscoe Ames and his wife when they headed out. They came across my land and my men said they had sold out and were going back east. The boys didn't get who they said he sold to. Thought we'd ride over and meet my new neighbors," McCloud said.

"I bought the place," Rivers said.

McCloud was shocked and it showed. "I don't mean to act surprised, but I thought you were a cowhand for Peters up in Colorado," McCloud said.

"I was, but now I own this place."

McCloud noticed the horses in the corral and let his eyes roam the lot, eleven in all. "You've got some good looking young mares," McCloud said.

"Yep. Bought them off Peters," Rivers responded.

"Well, I guess this just proves you ought not figure a man until you get him figured," McCloud said with a smile and extended his hand down from the saddle to reach for Rivers' hand. "If I can ever be a neighbor to you, let me know."

Rivers took his hand in another one of those strength battles and returned the smile, forced and riding below two eyes that looked into McCloud's soul. "The same goes for me," Rivers said.

McCloud and his foreman had ridden off that day without looking back. As Rivers watched them leave, he couldn't help but think of the reasons he had to dislike his father. He could not forget the words of his mother when she told him McCloud was a good man whom she had loved all her life. Maybe time would prove his mother right, but for the moment he still enjoyed not liking the man.

Three weeks later what he had been longing for came to pass. Nighthawk, Durham, and Mary came riding up to the ranch with a string of horses in tow. Four riders from the Crooked Wind rode with them. The commotion outside alarmed Rivers and he rushed out to see the happy band dismounting.

"Rivers," Mary shouted. She rushed to meet him and they embraced with Rivers swinging her around in a circle, her feet flying.

"You look so good Mary," Rivers whispered to her. "Did these boys take good care of you?"

"I've never felt safer in all my life. Mr. Durham has been my personal bodyguard and friend," she said.

Rivers turned to look at his two close friends and saw the pride they felt in accomplishing their mission. He was proud of them too. Roscoe

Durham was beaming with the words Mary had used to describe him.

"Did you folks have any trouble?" Rivers asked.

"Nope," Durham replied. "Nighthawk knows what he is doing and we skirted around all the possible trouble."

It was unusual for Nighthawk to kid, but he smiled and said, "The only trouble I had was getting any work out of Durham. He said you told him to keep anything from happening to your sister and he was going to do that. I could do everything else."

"It looks like you brought me more than ten horses. Where did the others come from?" Rivers asked.

"The men who delivered them to the ranch said Amos Griggs told them to tell you he felt ashamed sending only ten after his mares dropped their young horses sired by your stallion. He said he was going to be the envy of his parts when it came to horses. Said he was oblidged to you and he felt obligated to send you five extra," Nighthawk said.

Rivers looked at the horses and marveled at the soundness and beauty of the fifteen head of young mares. He thought, Amos Griggs is a white man to be trusted.

"Mary, you remember Goldy," Rivers said as he directed his sister toward his friend.

"We're proud you are here," Goldy said as he put his hand out to shake hers.

"Mary, this is Loleta Mesa, Pablo's wife. She cooks for us and she will show you your room," Rivers said as he motioned for the men to get her gear and take it inside.

"I am so proud to have another woman on this place," Loleta said. "Come with me and I will show you your room."

The women left and Rivers turned to the men who had traveled with the group. "I appreciate you men making this trip and taking care of my sister and horses. I would like for you to stay here and work with me. I won't hold it against you if you've got reasons to return."

"We told them before we left you might want them to stay, and they came along ready to do that if you wanted," Durham said.

"What about it men?" Rivers asked.

The four nodded agreement and said they were hoping Rivers would want them to stay.

"Then it's settled. Get my horses in the corral, your gear in the bunkhouse, and we will go over the details with you later.

The men left, following his orders. Rivers turned to his three friends and said, "Let's go up to the porch and get caught up."

As the men talked of the new horse barn, branding of cattle, the deal Rivers had made with the Kiowa, and the lack of any contact with the Bar M and Matthew McCloud, Mary finally found some solitude sitting on the edge of her new bed and looking out the window at her new home. In the background she could hear the talking and occasional laughter from her brother and friends on the porch. The sound was distant as her mind drew other things close.

He hasn't used the name Star yet, she thought. Mary is fine. She indulged in a selfish moment. She was finally home. She was with the most special person in her life, Tse-quo-ni. The sorrows and abuse of her people in Georgia seemed far away. The humbling experience of living in the pigsty the white people called the glorious provision for the Cherokee people of the Indian Territory was behind her. For the first time in two years she felt alive and had hope. Her heart would sing her mother's song of hope tonight.

Later in the evening, after supper, Rivers and Mary sat alone on the porch and talked.

"Tse-quo-ni, have you found the man who is your father?" Mary asked.

"Yes, No-qui-si, I have met him. He is a big man who seems to be above the hard feelings I have for him. I can't get it out of my mind that he lied to my mother. You have known for some time that I have terrible battles inside of me about the way the white people have treated our people. I hate to say it to you, but I have hatred in my heart for your father. I do not expect you to understand me and I am sorry for saying it in your presence. It is not fair of me. I also have hard feelings about the way our people allowed the white people to rob them of their old ways. But then, had it not been for the way things happened, I would not have you. It can not all be bad because you are the most powerful gift I have," Rivers spurted out in an unusual flow of words.

"You do not have to apologize for your feelings. If I were you, I might have the same feelings. It is hard for me to explain the closeness I had with our mother and the distance I too felt between me and my father. It was like I represented something he did not like. I came to believe it was because I was so much like mother and he resented the love she never gave him," Mary said.

"You are probably right," Rivers said. "What matters is we are here together and our lives are still before us. It means so much to me to have you here."

"To me too, brother. I love you so much," Mary said.

"I do not know how things will develop between me and Matthew McCloud. I guess time will tell that story."

"I'm glad you called me No-qui-si. "It is your name for me as Tse-quo-ni is mine for you."

"For the people who could hear us, we will be Rivers and Mary. We must live in the white man's world. But we will always be Cherokee and when we have our times alone, you will always be my little No-qui-si."

26

Things had been a buzz inside Matthew McCloud's family after he and Cutler returned with the news that the cowhand named Rivers had bought Ames ranch. When Toby and Tyler heard it, the twins almost went crazy. They had hatred for the man who backed them down and talked to them with disrespect.

They found the right time and went to their mother with the news. The three had been talking for some time about how they could get rid of Matthew McCloud and leave them owners of the ranch. While the twins were mean and unbridled, their mother was shrewd and evil. Her marriage to McCloud and moving to this territory was for one purpose only. Ultimately she planned to be a big person and give opportunity to her sons. She had no scruples and less love for Matthew McCloud.

A plan was carefully thought out and the new owner of the Ames ranch came into play in a special way. The boys could accomplish the task of ridding themselves of Matthew McCloud and at the same time get even with the man named Rivers. The plan had taken about two months to mature in their minds. It was ushered into action early on a Tuesday morning.

Toby and Tyler McCloud sprinted into the ranch yard, pulled their horses to sliding stops, hailed Bob Cutler, and rushed into the ranch house to talk with Matthew McCloud.

"Somebody run a bunch of our cattle off our range and onto the ranch the man named Rivers bought," Toby told the two men. "Looks to be about forty head and we picked up the tracks of two riders pushing them.

You told us to stay away from over there. So we backed off and came to tell you. I knew it would come too something like this. I don't trust that man."

Tyler was offering his agreement as Toby spoke.

"You did right coming and telling us," Matthew said. "Me and Bob will ride out and get to the bottom if it. Where did they cross over?"

"It was up on the high ground where the big ravine runs off the ranch and onto their land," Tyler said.

"Well, ya'll find you something else to do. We'll handle this," Matthew said.

The boys left and Cutler looked at his boss and asked, "What do you make of this?"

"I don't know. I thought this man Rivers was straight, even if he is rough. We'll just have to go out there and sort it out."

The two men went out, saddled up, and rode toward the place the twins had directed them.

They found the trail of the cattle easily and followed it. They moved slowly and observed whoever moved the cattle did the same. They probably did so to avoid any dust that could be observed from a distance. It also kept down the noise the cattle would make in a hurried drive.

McCloud and Cutler were sure the rustlers would keep a lookout on their back trail so they stopped to study the land in front of them when they had to move over any high ground. When they did move and skyline themselves, they did so quickly. They didn't want to be an easy target for someone hiding out.

It was obvious the rustlers were taking the cattle onto the ranch owned by Rivers. He couldn't figure out why a man like Rivers would steal his cattle and leave such a clear trail. He had more questions about Rivers than he could answer anyway. He couldn't pinpoint what it was about the man that bothered him so much. The young man had a self assurance he admired. He couldn't help but admire the man's attitude. It reminded him of himself in his younger years. Rivers reflected no back-up at all. There was something in his eyes and the way he looked at McCloud that caused his hair to stand up on his neck. It was almost like he had something against him. Now the trail of rustled cattle was leading to his ranch. Maybe the man was a thief and that was what bothered McCloud. Well, McCloud thought, I'll rope that bronc when I get to it.

The trail led to a seep at the base of some rocks and they saw where the cattle had finished off the small amount of rain runoff that occasionally was held there. A study of the tracks revealed two horsemen were driving the cattle. He could tell the tracks were at least two days old by the dried mud in the seep. The rustlers probably had the cattle holed up somewhere so they could change the brands. If it was Rivers, they would go back and get more men before they had a showdown.

The cattle trail moved away from the river. It followed a long narrow valley east. It took them an hour to get to where the trail led back northwest and then it cut due north. After another hour they heard the cattle. They may not be mine, McCloud thought.

"Let's move careful Bob and get close enough to see what's going on," McCloud said.

"I think we better get off these horses," Cutler said. "If we run into trouble, we better be ready to shoot."

They dismounted and walked up a runoff ditch covered with scrub brush. The ditch wound its way to the top of a ridge. The sound of cattle was getting louder. When they got to the top, they crawled until they could see off the other side. The cattle were there, held in place in a narrow ravine by poles forming gates on each end.

They studied the layout. There was no sign of guards. They waited a while, thinking through their next move.

McCloud whispered to Cutler, "If we can slip down there and remove the poles on this end, we can start the cattle walking toward home. If we get them started, I think they will take it from there."

"It's worth a try," Cutler said.

Both men moved down to the pole gate and started to lift the top pole. It was the last thing they did. The sound of the rifles reached their ears a split second after the bullets hit them and threw them to the ground. Both men were shot in the back.

Then it was quiet, except for the shuffling and bawling of the cattle.

27

Rivers was scouting the easternmost part of his ranch when he discovered the tracks of a sizeable herd of cattle. He backtracked the herd and found where they had come off McCloud's ranch. He found tracks of two horses. It was obvious the cattle were being driven.

He turned back toward the place where he first discovered the tracks and then continued to follow the trail. He thought, why would anybody be driving McCloud's cattle onto my range? The obvious answer spelled trouble however you read it.

The tracks were no more than a couple of days old. Rivers moved carefully, fully aware he could find trouble over the next hill. About an hour later he rode into the narrow cuts through the high ground and came up on the holding pen for the cattle. He purposely stayed at a distance. He dismounted and crawled up to a vantage point where he could glass the area. There appeared to be about fifty head of cattle closed inside a narrow cut by pole gates on both ends. He saw no sign of anybody guarding the cattle. That did not mean they were not there. Too many places existed up close where somebody could be hiding with a rifle. It would be easy for a person to say the reason he got killed was because he got caught rustling cattle. He decided to back off and go get Goldy. Together they could get a closer look at the site.

"I figure somebody is trying to set me up to give McCloud a reason to come after me," Rivers said, having explained to Goldy about the cattle.

"Could be. It don't make sense though. He just don't shape up to be that kind a man," Goldy said.

"He don't fool me none. If he wasn't that kind, then he'd put some reins on them two boys of his. I believe he's after me. He's wanted this place real bad," Rivers said.

"What you figure on doing?"

"I want you to ride out there with me. If nobody's around, we'll head the cattle back onto McCoud's range."

"What if somebody is with them and they are waiting on us/" Goldy asked.

"We'll teach them a lesson," Rivers said.

The two rode out and were about a mile from the place where the cattle were being held when two rifle shots rang out. The shots were so close together they almost sounded as one. Rivers and Goldy pulled up and listened for more. Sounds can fool you, but these sounded as if they came from the direction they were headed. They held their position for a few minutes and after hearing nothing else, moved out carefully.

They slowly worked their way to a place where they could belly up and see the makeshift corral. When Rivers put his glass on it he immediately saw the two bodies sprawled on the ground.

"Two men are down at the gate," Rivers whispered. "They ain't moving. Let's check it out before we go down."

Goldy had his eye glass out and they both checked the area closely.

"I don't see nothing," Goldy said. "Let me slip around to the right and check the high ground out. I figure that's where the shots came from. I'll work my way out on that point over yonder," pointing to a place directly in front of the corral. "I'll signal you if it is clear."

"Be careful," Rivers said.

Goldy backed down below the peak of the high ground and sneaked his way along. About twenty minutes later he came up on a place where two horses had recently been tied up. The droppings and places where they had cropped grass were fresh. He looked up the rise and saw some scuff marks where somebody had gone up and down the hill. He worked his way up and came out on a flat place surrounded by waist high rocks.

The sign was clear. Whoever did the shooting did it from here. Tracks were all over the soft soil and four cigarette butts were on the ground. They were the type of small mexican cigars about the size of a cigarette. He picked them up and slipped then into his shirt pocket.

After surveying the area carefully and seeing nothing to alarm him, he walked to the place he pointed out to Rivers and waved him on down.

They got to the corral at about the same time. Rivers dismounted first and went straight to the fallen men. While he did so, Goldy had his rifle trained on the high ground just in case they had missed seeing anybody.

"This one is McCloud," Rivers said in a surprised voice. He looked at the ashen face of his father without emotion. He turned to roll the other man over and was equally surprised. "It's his foreman," he continued. "It don't make sense."

He felt for a pulse in the foreman's neck and found none. "He's dead." He turned back to McCloud and felt for a pulse. "He's still alive," he exclaimed. He gently rolled him over. "He was shot in the back and it came out on the front of his chest just below his right shoulder. He's lost a lot of blood. I'm going to see if I can stop the bleeding," Rivers said.

He got some cloth from his saddle bags and tore some small pieces he pushed into the entrance and exit wounds. He tied them in place with longer strips. He then rolled McCloud over on his back and lifted his head a mite to pour a little water from his canteen into the wounded man's mouth. McCloud was unconscious, near death.

"We've got to get him to the ranch," Rivers said. "You keep watch while I rig a travois. It's the only way I can think of to move him in his condition."

He got busy hacking down two pole saplings. The big blade on his knife was better than an axe. He tied a blanket to the poles and tied the long ends of the poles to both sides of McCloud's horse. Rivers and Goldy lifted McCloud onto the blanket. They put the dead body of Bob Colter across his saddle and tied him there.

"I'm going to head out for the ranch," Rivers said. "Open the corral gate and head the cattle back toward the McCloud range. I figure they'll do the rest on their own. Then come back and try to remove as much of our sign as you can, especially the travois. Before they could come after me for stealing cattle, now they can add murder to it."

"I'll get it done. You be careful and I'll see you at the ranch," Goldy said.

Rivers was right. Once Goldy got the cattle moving they traveled right along without being pushed. He followed along for a spell and then returned to work on the sign.

Rivers made it pretty easy. McCloud was unconscious and unaware of the jolting of the travois. He got to the ranch about two hours later and with the help of the ranch hands moved McCloud inside and placed him on his bed.

"Lolita, you and Mary clean his wounds and do what you can for him," Rivers said. "I'll be back to explain in a minute."

Rivers went to where the ranch hands were gathered out front. "Get rid of the travois. Wrap Colter's body in blankets and take him up the hill to the thicket and bury him. Cover the ground good with leaves and sticks when you cover him up. Take the two horses and put them in the back stalls. Stash the saddles up in the barn under some hay. Don't say a word to anybody about this. When I get time, I will explain it all to you. Just trust me and do as I say," Rivers ordered.

The men got busy and Rivers went back inside. The women had already bathed McCloud's wounds, put some herbal medicine into them, and redressed them. They were pouring a little water into his mouth when Rivers walked in.

"The bleeding has stopped," Mary said.

"If he does not get an infection or if some vital organ was not damaged, he might live," Lolita said. "He was fortunate the bullet went all the way through him."

Rivers looked at McCloud. The big man seemed so helpless and hopeless. The loss of blood left him pale. His breathing was shallow, but steady. You can never tell, Rivers thought. He might just live.

He walked out on the porch and sat down to let the events of his day sink in. He had not been there long when Goldy rode up and dismounted. He stepped up on the porch and plopped down beside Rivers.

Rivers told him of McCloud's condition and the orders he had given the men. Goldy assured him all anybody could find up at the place where it all happened would be the tracks of cattle that must have wandered over on them and then wandered back.

"Let me show you what I found where the shooters waited on them," Goldy said. He pulled the little cigar butts from his pocket. "There's a lot of people who smoke these things. I know of two for sure."

"McCloud's boys smoke them don't they?"

"Yep. The first thing I thought about," Goldy said.

"That's crazy. Why would they shoot their father?"

"Beats me. The boot tracks up there seemed to fit their size too."

"Don't say anything about this. If he makes it, I'll wait for the right time to tell him. In the meantime, we need to get ready for visitors. As soon as they miss him, somebody will come looking for him."

They came around noon the next day. Toby and Tyler led a group of riders into the ranch yard. One of Rivers' hands had ridden in to give them the warning. Rivers had his men positioned to cover anything that could take place.

They rode in rapidly and were met by Rivers, Durham, Night Hawk, and Goldy as they walked down off the porch. One of the twins blared out in an angry voice, "My father and Bob Cutler are missing and we think you had something to do with it."

"If they are missing, how do you know anybody had anything to do with it?" Rivers asked.

"Me and Toby found a trail where some of our cattle had been driven onto your land. We were told to stay off your land. So we went and told our father. He told us to leave it alone and he and Cutler would check it out. That was yesterday morning. We haven't seen them since," Tyler said.

"Did you find any of your cattle on my land?"

Tyler was hesitant to answer, but finally said, "No."

"Did you find any trace of your father and Cutler on my land?"

"No."

"Then what makes you think we had anything to do with it?"

"All we know is we saw where you or some of your men had driven cattle off our range onto yours. They went to check it out and are missing. If you killed them, you are going to hang," Toby chimed in.

"Now hold it a minute. You ride up to my ranch accusing me of stealing your cattle and killing two men without a notion of what you are talking about," Rivers said. "Listen to me. I am going to say this once. We had nothing to do with driving your cattle or doing any harm to your father and Cutler."

"I don't believe you," Tyler said.

Before anyone could react, Rivers reached up and pulled Tyler from his saddle and placed his knife at the startled twin's neck. "Now everybody stay real still," Rivers said. "We don't want to hurt any of you cowhands. I've got enough guns on you right now to empty every saddle."

The riders calmed down and realized they were in a bad situation. Toby looked like he wanted to come to his brother's rescue, but he wasn't ready to die doing it.

"You have accused me of stealing and harming two men," Rivers said to Tyler. "I ought to cut your throat. I don't aim to spend my time on this ranch fighting with you folks. Don't you ever set foot on my place again. Do you understand?"

"Tyler felt the blade of the knife clearly and was careful when he mumbled, "Uh-huh." Beads of sweat were rolling down his face.

Rivers released his grasp on him and motioned for him to mount up. He then said, "Get off my land."

They turned to ride out. One of the riders held behind and turned back to face Rivers. "My name is Boggs. Don't think this was our idea. Them boys are doing some crazy things right now. We all were close to McCloud and Cutler. This is a puzzle to us. Just wanted you to know it wasn't our idea to ride over here."

"Thanks," Rivers said. "If I was you, I'd keep an eye on them two boys."

"We aim to. Hope there ain't no hard feelings. If I was you, I'd stay off our place til this cools down and we know what's going on. After today, the boys will probably be looking for a chance to kill you," Boggs said.

"Don't you worry. We don't have no reason to come over there."

Boggs turned and rode away.

28

The only change in Matthew McCloud's condition was an occasional incoherent mumbling. He had some infection and was very feverish. Three days had passed.

Mary had been almost a constant companion to McCloud, sitting by his bedside bathing his hot face with cold cloths. She had changed his dressings often and applied more herbal ointments to his wounds. She was very careful in moving him to avoid starting up his bleeding. Rivers was amazed at her ability to care for the wounded man. It made him proud of her.

Early on the morning of the fourth day Mary hurried into the kitchen where Rivers was pouring himself a cup of coffee.

"He's awake," she said. "At least he has his eyes open."

"Has he said anything?"

"No," Mary replied.

Rivers took his coffee and walked to the room, followed by Mary. Matthew McCloud had his eyes open in a strange look of bewilderment.

"Take it easy," Rivers said. "You've been shot and you have lost a lot of blood. You haven't bled any in three days, but if you move around you could start it again."

McCloud blinked his eyes and tried to speak.

"You are going to be fine if we can get by the infection and fever. Close your eyes and try to sleep," Rivers said.

McCloud's expression did not change. His eyes appeared to be set. Then it dawned upon him McCloud's eyes were locked on Mary.

Rivers motioned for Mary to leave and he watched McCloud's eyes follow her to the door. He leaned over McCloud and spoke in a low voice. "You're going to have to help us. Make up your mind you are going to live. You are at my ranch and we will take care of you until you can go home. Now close your eyes and sleep."

McCloud blinked his eyes a couple of times and then closed them. He was breathing easily. Rivers gently touched his face and felt the heat of the fever. The fever has to break for him to have a chance, Rivers thought.

It broke during the following night. Mary woke Rivers to come help her. McCloud was pouring perspiration and his clothing and bed were soaked. They carefully changed him and the bed clothes beneath him. Mary left the room and Rivers was there with him alone.

McCloud looked up at him in the dim lamplight and asked, "Where am I?"

"You are at my ranch. I found you almost five days ago," Rivers said.

"Who shot me?"

"We'll talk about it later."

"What about Cutler?"

"Right now you've got to rest. You must let your wounds heal," Rivers said.

"Has there been a woman taking care of me?"

Rivers chuckled and said, "She's not a woman yet. My little sister has been looking after you. Why do you ask about her?"

"Oh, it don't matter. I thought it was somebody else," McCloud said. "What's her name?" he mustered enough strength to ask.

"Mary."

McCloud's eyes widened for a moment and then he closed them as he drifted off.

Afterwards Rivers cautioned Mary about talking with McCloud. He wanted to bring up the subject of their relationship on his own.

The next morning Rivers went into the room with McCloud to find

Mary spooning some broth down him. McCloud looked stronger and was wide awake. McCloud looked in Rivers direction when he entered and half nodded in his direction between the spoonfuls of broth. When Mary finished, she wiped his mouth and left the room.

"How old is your sister?" McCloud asked. "I asked her and she won't talk to me."

"She's fifteen," Rivers said.

"I know it's crazy, but she reminds me of someone I knew a long time ago," McCloud said.

"Who does she remind you of?" Rivers asked.

"When I was nineteen I fell in love with a young woman who was a Cherokee Indian. My family lived in Georgia at the time. Your sister is the spitting image of the woman I loved. I know it sounds crazy to you, but she looks so much like her I thought I was dead when I woke up and saw her for the first time."

Rivers began to fish a little and said, "This woman you loved must have jilted you since you don't have her with you now."

"In a way I guess she did. I ain't told nobody about this in a long time. It took me a long time to get over her. No. I'm lying. I ain't ever got over her," McCloud said.

"What happened?"

"My father upped and moved us to Texas all of a sudden. We were planning on getting married. I promised her I would come back and get her as soon as we got settled . It took me four months to get back. When I did, I found out she was already married to another man."

Rivers was taking this all in with an interest McCloud had no way of perceiving. "Did you talk to her when you went back?"

"No. I asked about her when I got pretty close. When I learned she was married, I just went all to hell. I was heartbroken, mad, and disappointed all at the same time. I knew the boy she married and he wasn't worth killing. I started to go kill him and take her, but then I figured if she wanted him, she could have him. I thought I knew her better than that. She said she loved me and would wait for me. She's the only woman

I have ever loved. I don't guess I'll ever get over it."

"What about the woman you are married to now. Don't you love her?"

"Naw. That's another story. She caught me in a weak moment and used her body and high ways to trap me," McCloud said.

"How'd she do that?"

"Her father was tight with the Spanish leaders. My father was too. That's how I got the land my ranch is on. She used her influence and a strong application of her physical beauty to influence me that marrying her was the answer. Now I hadn't had a lot of experience in them things. She trapped me. I have regretted it ever since," McCloud said.

"We have talked way too much with you as weak as you are. You get some rest and we will finish this later," Rivers said.

"I want to thank you for taking care of me," McCloud said.

"Don't mention it. You would have done the same for me wouldn't you?"

"Yes. I would."

Rivers walked out with his mind spinning. He went back for my mother, he thought.

29

Rivers spent a sleepless night thinking back over all Matthew McCloud said about his mother. It bothered him to think McCloud and his mother spent their lives loving one another and did not get to spend it together. He was having a hard time hanging on to the bitterness he had held since learning about McCloud being his father. He purposely stayed away from McCloud for a couple of days. He was trying to figure out how to tell him about his own relationship to him and the fact his two sons tried to kill him.

McCloud was getting stronger and was sitting in a chair when Rivers walked into the room.

"Looks like you are feeling better," Rivers said.

"I am, but I am weak as a new born calf," McCloud said.

"Do you feel strong enough to talk a spell? I've got a lot to tell you," Rivers said.

"I've been hoping you would come. I've got a lot to ask you too," McCloud said.

"Why don't you go first. Ask me whatever you need to," Rivers said.

"Who shot me and what happened to Cutler?"

"We found these where you were shot. Found them up in the rocks where the shooting came from." Rivers held out the small cigar butts. "Figured you'd recognize them. I saw your sons smoking them," Rivers said. "Cutler was dead when we got to you. Probably died immediately. They thought you were dead. They didn't come down to check their work."

"It don't surprise me none. They brought the news about our cattle being driven onto your land. It was a trap all the time. Them boys are mean through and through, and their mama is meaner than both of them."

"I know it has to be rough on you knowing your own sons were trying to kill you and did kill your good friend," Rivers said.

"Oh, I figured you knew. They ain't my sons. At their mother's insistence I let them take on my name. I met their mother while I was on a trip to Texas to buy some horses. She was a looker and could charm a rattlesnake. I always said I would never get married. Before I knew it, I was. It was a foolish thing. I brought her and them boys, eleven years old at the time, back here. I didn't learn til later they had hung her daddy in Texas for killing a man. He had the reputation of doing anything for a dollar. Well, Suella is a whole lot like him. My getting shot was probably her idea. She can be fearsome mean," McCloud said. "She worked it so them boys could take my name. Right now they can see themselves sitting on a pile of money. I have worked hard at the Bar M and I have been very successful. With me dead it's all theirs."

Rivers listened to McCloud talk and was in shock. He didn't let it show. It seemed like every time he turned around he was learning things about his father that made him like him and feel sorry for him.

"We buried Cutler back behind the house. We felt like it would be just a matter of time before somebody from your ranch came looking. They came three days back. The twins and about eight riders came calling. The twins were trying to lay blame on us. We had run your cattle back onto the Bar M and erased all the sign of you and Cutler being shot up there. They don't have any bodies to claim murder and they found no Bar M cattle on our place. I sent them packing. One of your men, named Boggs, stayed behind a minute and told us the men on the ranch didn't know what to think. They are very loyal to you. I told them to keep an eye on the twins," Rivers said.

"You've been mighty good to me," McCloud said. "If you can give me a couple of weeks to get my strength back, I'll get out of your hair. I plan to go home and send my wife and them boys packing."

"Do you think they will just up and leave because you tell them to? If they find out you are alive, they will kill you for sure," Rivers said.

"Yep. I don't know how I will handle it. But when the time comes, I'll get it done."

"You said a while ago you had never planned on getting married. Why was that?"

"I don't know why you are so interested in that, but it was the truth. It's a long story. One I've never told nobody. My family knew way back because they had to nurse me through some tough days," McCloud said.

"You can talk to me about it. I'd like to hear your story," Rivers said.

"I'm not sure I can. I ain't talked about it for so long. But I can promise you there ain't been a day pass without me thinking about it."

"It must be something powerful to stay with you so long."

"It is. As I said, I fell in love with a beautiful young Cherokee girl when we lived back in Georgia. It was a sudden thing. My folks liked her. Our moving didn't have anything to do with her being an Indian. We were both young and didn't know much about courting. However, we loved each other. Or so I thought," McCloud spilled out.

"To be honest, I could never love a woman like I loved her. That's why I said I would never marry. Suella used her magic and tricked this old boy. I don't have nobody to blame for that but me," McCloud said.

Rivers listened to McCloud and felt a ton of anger and resentment peel off his heart. He carefully hid his emotions. Today was not the time to tell him the rest of the story. He wanted to think through how he was going to handle the things at the Bar M for his father. What? Did I use the word father, he thought. He smiled to himself. Just to know that McCloud had not lied to his mother brought much relief.

"We've talked enough for one day. I've got a ranch to run. We will do some more talking tomorrow. I want you to know it does not seem fair that two people who loved each other could not spend their lives together," Rivers said.

"I just can't figure out why she didn't wait for me," McCloud answered.

"You won't understand until you know. Maybe there was a reason that would help you to understand. We'll talk tomorrow," Rivers said as he stood and walked out.

30

The night was a sleepless one for Rivers. He spent it going from one scenario to another, trying to figure out how he would disclose to McCloud the truth about his mother and the more immediate truth of McCloud being his father. Late in the night Rivers decided he would do it just as his mother asked.

After breakfast Rivers walked into the room where McCloud was staying and found him sitting in a chair. He looked much stronger. Rivers sat on the bed next to him.

"I was asked to give you this," Rivers said as he extended the small broach given to him by his mother.

McCloud reached to take it and he lifted it so he could see it better. His hands began to shake.

"Where did you get this?" McCloud asked.

"It was given to me along with the request to find you and tell you the woman who possessed it had loved you all her life. She gave it to me shortly before she died," Rivers said.

Tears welled up in McCloud's eyes and spilled down his cheeks. He pulled the broach close to his heart and held it there with both hands. Then he began to weep. Years of a broken heart flooded out of the big man.

Rivers sat quietly. It was hard for him to watch. He was not certain how he felt about him. But he was sure McCloud had loved his mother

After what seemed like an eternity to Rivers, McCloud began to gain control of his emotions.

"You said she was dead. How did she die?"

"I don't know. I was not with her. She had been sick with something that made it hard for her to breathe," Rivers said.

"How did you come to know her?"

"I am known as Rivers. My real name is Tse-quo-ni. I am a Cherokee warrior from the high mountains where the sun appears," Rivers said. "I knew the woman well. She told me her story just before she died. It is much like yours. She told me of your deep love for each other and your plans to be married. She also told me of your sudden move west and your promise to return for her.

"It is here your stories are different. She never knew you returned for her. She learned soon after you left that she was going to have a baby. She waited and hoped for your return. She made a decision to avoid the embarrassment for her unborn child. It was not for her, but her child. She married Franklin Adair. She never told him she was with child before their marriage or after. She spent her life with a man she did not love, bore him three other children, and lay on her death bed thinking of you," Rivers said.

McCloud began to weep again. This episode was more intense than the first. After a while the crying subsided and realization began to sink in.

"If what you tell me is true, then I have a child," McCloud said. "Did the child live?"

"The woman you loved had four children. I am her oldest child," Rivers said, without emotion though his heart was racing. He then sat quietly and watched his words sink in with McCloud.

"Are you telling me you are my son?"

"I am telling you I am her oldest child," Rivers said. "That is all I will say. I have spent my entire life without a father. My being here has nothing to do with a search for a father. I am simply following my mother's wishes."

"Rivers, you are my son," McCloud said with searching eyes.

"Please do not start this," Rivers said. "My sister Mary, who has been caring for you, is the youngest child in my family."

"That's why she reminded me so much of her." McCloud said. "You have something of me and your mother in your looks. That's why I always felt like somebody was standing on my grave every time I was around you. I couldn't figure it out. Rivers, you've got to believe I didn't know about you. I would have whipped everybody in Georgia and brought you and your mother with me."

"It is meaningless now," Rivers said. "If it means anything to you, I find joy in you and my mother loving each other and sorrow in the fact you lived separate miserable lives."

"Please tell me more about your mother and your life," McCloud said.

"No. There will be time for that," Rivers said.

31

When Rivers came to the table for breakfast the next morning Mary was waiting on him.

"You must talk with him," Mary said. "He has been begging me to talk to him and asking me all kinds of questions. He wants to know of your life and mother's life. He soaks up anything he can learn about us."

"I will speak with him after breakfast," Rivers said.

When he finished eating he walked to McCloud's room and found him dressed in a shirt and pants. It was the first time since being brought to the ranch.

"Good morning," Rivers said. "You look like you are getting stronger each day."

"I am. I am walking a few steps on wobbly legs, but I am getting better thanks to you and Mary," McCloud said. "I'm proud you came. I've been wanting to talk with you desperately since our conversation yesterday. I wish you knew how happy it makes me to learn you are my son."

"I do not want to talk about that," Rivers said. He noticed the frown on McCloud's face and his obvious hurt in Rivers response. "The time will come when we will talk. The immediate need is to get you well and back to your ranch."

"You give me a couple of more weeks and I'll get out of here," McCloud said, hurt by Rivers' reluctance to talk about their relationship. "I'll go home and get Suella and the twins off the place. That will be my first job."

"You won't have to do that," Rivers replied. "I plan on doing that for you."

"You can't do that. It ain't your business," McCloud said.

"Oh yes it is. They made it my business when they tried to set me up with your death," Rivers said. "They came here the day after we brought you here, trying to pin your disappearance on me."

"You don't know how mean the three of them are. I can't let you get involved," McCloud said.

"You can't keep me from it," Rivers replied. "All I want you to do is get well and get out of my house," Rivers continued with a faint smile.

"If my boys think you had something to do with all this, it will be dangerous for you to go to my ranch," McCloud said.

"All they know now is you and Cutler are missing. I've got a plan working in my mind on how to get to your ranch and clear them out. At some point I will need your help," Rivers said.

"I don't want you to get hurt," McCloud said.

Rivers chuckled and said, "People have been trying to hurt me all my life. I ain't all that easy to hurt. I want you to be able to go home. I can't let you go in a weak condition and face them people. They would kill you before you could get anything done. You just relax and let me handle it."

"You do have a lot of me in you, Rivers. Especially the hard head," McCloud said.

"No. I'm sorry. There ain't much of you in me," Rivers said as he got up and walked out.

He's a hard man, McCloud thought as he watched him leave. I guess I would be too. In spite of the hurt in Rivers words, the big man found some space for pride in his son.

32

Rivers went outside and found Goldy, Durham, and Nighthawk lounging around waiting on him. He walked over to them and asked, "Does the McCloud ranch still have some of their cattle on the north range by the river?"

"They sure do," Goldy replied. "They are about a mile inside their property."

"I've got a job for you. Do you know how many men they have watching the cattle?"

"I rode over to where I could see them yesterday. I made out three men with the cattle," Goldy said.

"I want you to ride out this afternoon and bring their riders here," Rivers said. "Don't hurt them. I'm sure you'll have to make them come. Do you think you can do that?"

"It won't be a problem," Nighthawk replied. "You must have a plan working."

"I do. If it goes the way I've got it planned, we'll have McCloud back on his ranch soon. After you get his men here and I let them see their boss, I'm going to go over and invite his wife and the twins to leave. I'll want the three of you to go with me," Rivers said.

"You bet," Goldy said. "It'll be a pleasure."

Durham and Nighthawk nodded their agreement.

"I might as well go ahead and tell you men about Matthew McCloud and why I am doing this," Rivers said. "It is a long story and I don't have time to fill in all the details. My mother you already know was a Cherokee.

She fell in love with Matthew McCloud back in Georgia. McCloud's family moved west before they could be married and after they left my mother realized she was going to have a baby. She married someone else to avoid the embarrassment. She truly loved McCloud. The main reason I came here was to keep a promise to my mother. Matthew McCloud is my father.

"Well, I'll be dog," Goldy replied

"I have come to believe Matthew McCloud is not a lying white man," Rivers said. "He went back for my mother only to find her married to another man. She never knew he came. I have learned he lived his life loving only my mother. It helps to know the twins are not his children. I am going to help him get rid of his wife and the boys and then I will get him home to his ranch. I really don't know how I feel about him as my father. Up to now I have just been keeping my mother's wishes."

"It's a good reason to help him," Goldy said. "But we don't need one. We trust you. We'll have the McCloud hands here before dark."

They got their horses and rode out. They easily found the McCloud cattle and pulled up in some brush to check the situation out and make their plans. They were about a quarter of a mile away from the cattle. After glassing the area for a spell they decided there were only two McCloud ranch hands guarding the cattle.

The area where the cattle were being held was a flat stretch running back from the river. The two riders moved back and forth along the eastern flank of the cattle, allowing the river to contain them on the western side. The riders rode separately and passed each other about every thirty minutes.

"Looks to me like the best place to get them will be when they are alone at each end," Goldy said. "Course we could just ride out there and chance it, but they might be a little trigger happy after all thats happened."

"I think you are right," Nighthawk said. "Why don't I ride around to the other end of the herd and get one of them there. You could slip down by the river on this end and be waiting on the other one."

"How long do you figure it will take you to get around there?"

"I've been watching them. They just passed each other. If they keep up the same pace, I should be ready for mine by the time they pass three more times," Nighthawk said.

"Then get going. I'll leave my horse here with Durham and slip down on foot. Remember, don't shoot unless you have to," Goldy said.

"I got it," Nighthawk said as he backed out of the brush and headed for his horse.

Goldy mapped out his plan and route down to the river. Both riders had been going clear to the river bank before they turned around. He figured the turn around point was his best bet.

The riders were about to pass each other again by the time Goldy slipped out of his position and began to work his way down to the river. He didn't want to get there early and spook a horse before Nighthawk got into position. He had two more passes before he would take his man.

He stayed upstream along the river bank and watched the riders pass the second time. After the rider made his turn around and headed back he eased down the bank. He got to the turn around point and dropped down to the ground where the bank sloped quickly to the river. The rider would be right on top of him before he could see him. He was ready. He hoped Nighthawk was.

Goldy heard the saddle of the rider creak as he drew near and peaked over the bank to see the rider turning the horse.

"If you don't move or make a sound, you may live to see daylight tomorrow," Goldy said in a low but clear voice.

The rider tensed and held his horse still. "What do you want?"

"I want you to step down real careful like and keep your rifle in one hand with the barrel pointed straight up. If the barrel drops at all, you're dead," Goldy said.

The man did just as he was told and turned to face Goldy. "You are in big trouble," the man said. "There will be forty riders after you when they learn about this."

"Don't go jumping off no bluff yet," Goldy said as he took the man's rifle. "All I'm going to do is ask you to ride with me to our ranch. Rivers has somebody there who wants to talk with you. My partner will be bringing your buddy over here in a few minutes and we'll ride out. You ain't going to get hurt unless you do something crazy."

They looked up and saw Nighthawk coming their way with the other McCloud rider.

"Get on your horse and let's go to where I left mine," Goldy told the man.

They met where Durham was holding the horses and began the ride back to the ranch. They learned the names of the two men were Hesler and Adams. Both rode quietly and said nothing until they rode up to the ranch house. Rivers stepped down from the porch to meet them.

"You're going to have hell to pay for this," Adams said before Rivers could speak. "Everybody on the Bar M thinks you are behind the boss and Cutler's disappearance. This is going to settle it for sure."

"That's what Toby and Tyler want you to think and it is why you are here," Rivers said. "Do you men respect Matthew McCloud?"

"You bet we do," Hessler replied. "He's the best boss I ever had. Cutler is a good man too. There ain't a hand on the Bar M who wouldn't stand up for either of them."

"What about the twins?"

"It ain't the same with them. They're cut out of different stuff and most of the men are hanging on because they need work. We keep hoping the boss will come back," Adams said.

"Well, get down and come into the house with me. I've got somebody in there I want you to see," Rivers said as he turned and walked back inside.

Adams and Hesler dismounted and followed him. Rivers friends came behind. Rivers ushered the men into the room where Matthew McCloud was seated by the window.

"Howdy men. It's good to see you," McCloud said to the two shocked men.

"Mr. McCoud, we thought you was dead," Hesler said as the two men walked over close to their boss.

"By all rights I ought to be. If it hadn't been for Rivers and his men I would be," McCloud said.

"What happened?" Adams asked.

"The twins pushed some of our cattle over onto Rivers property and then came and told me some cattle had been stolen and they had trailed them to the edge of our range. I had told the boys to stay away from over here so I didn't think anything about it. Me and Cutler rode out to see what had happened. We cut the trail and followed the cattle. They were on Rivers' property and were being held in a makeshift corral. We'd just got down to turn them loose when we were ambushed. I woke up here about a week later and learned Cutler died right off. Rivers and his people have been nursing me all along," McCloud said.

"Who did it Boss?"

"It was the twins. Rivers men found the ambush sight where they waited on us and the ground was covered with them little black cigars they smoke," McCloud said.

"If that don't beat all," Adams said. "We'll go back to the ranch and take care of them for you."

"You won't have to do that," Rivers said. "McCloud has written out a note stating what you've just heard. He believes his wife and the boys are in this together. He wants them off the place now. I brought you here so you could see him alive and hear from him what he wants us to do. I am taking some of my men with me and tonight we are going to carry out his wishes. Without your help we might have a big fight on our hands before we ever get to them. I want you to slip us onto the ranch and into the bunkhouse where the hands are so we can tell them without Suella and the boys knowing we are there."

"We'll be glad to do that, but we'd rather take care of Mr. McCloud's problems ourselves," Hessler said.

"I want Rivers to do it," McCloud said. "I might as well tell you now. I'll be telling everybody I see from now on. Rivers is my son. I didn't know I had one until a few days ago. That's why I want him to handle it."

The two Bar M hands were astonished. They looked from McCloud to Rivers and back again. McCloud had a smile on his face and Rivers had his calm expressionless face on.

"Well, I'll be throwed and stomped," Adams said. "If that don't beat all."

Rivers interrupted the moment by saying, "We've got work to do men. Goldy, you get the note from McCloud and hang on to it. Let's go. It'll be good and dark by the time we get to the Bar M."

33

Rivers and his friends left their ranch with Hesler and Adams riding as one. They had returned the rifles belonging to the Bar M hands before leaving. The sun was getting low on the horizon when they passed the Bar M cattle.

Soon after they rode up on two Bar M riders coming to replace Hesler and Adams. They were accompanied by a big red dog trotting along beside them.

"Where ya'll headed?" an older man named Peden asked.

"I guess I better fill you in on what's about to happen," Hesler said. He told them the story of all the recent developments. The two riders listened with interest.

"You want us to turn around and ride with you?" Peden asked. "We'd be mighty proud to."

"That won't be necessary," Rivers said.

"Then ya'll stop back and tell us how it turns out," Peden said. "Is the boss going to be okay?"

"He'll be fine," Rivers replied.

They rode away from the two men and Rivers, riding beside Hesler, asked him, "What about the dog? Do they use it with the cattle?"

"Naw. That dog can smell an injun a mile off. They use him for that," Hesler said.

Rivers smiled to himself and thought, I must have more white blood in me than I figured.

The Bar M buildings were surrounded by a fence about a half mile out. The riders came up to one of two gates and Hesler called out as they approached.

"Who you got with you?" a voice inquired from the darkness.

"It's Rivers and three of his men," Hesler replied. "We'll tell you all about it when we get up close. Everything is okay."

"Ride on up," the voice said.

They came to the outside of the gate and Hesler told them the story and explained why Rivers and his men were there.

"You saw the boss?" the voice asked.

"Sure did. We are doing what he wants us to do," Hesler said. "Are the twins up at the house?"

"They were when we rode out a couple of hours ago. You want us to come in with you?"

"Nope," Hesler said. "We'll handle it. You might need to keep watch both ways for a while. You never know how these things will work out."

"We'll do it. Ya'll come on in and be careful." A figure emerged from the dark shadows and opened the gate.

"Rivers and the men rode through and headed on up to the ranch buildings. As they came closer they slowed to a walk and worked their way behind two large barns and up behind one of two bunk houses. The Bar M needed two to handle the sixty-plus riders they kept on the place.

They dismounted, tied their horses, and walked through the back door to one of the bunk houses. The big room was full of men. Some were playing cards, others working on tack, or just piled up here and there talking. They all looked up as the door opened and six men walked in.

"I got something to tell you fellers," Hesler said. "I want Adams to go over and bring the other men over before I do. I won't have to tell it but once."

Adams left by the back door.

One man asked, "What's going on and why are these men here?"

"I'll tell when Adams gets back with the others. Just relax a minute," Hesler said.

The door opened and the men began to file in. When they were all inside, Hesler began.

"Rivers sent these three," Hesler pointed to Goldy, Nighthawk, and Durham, "Out to our range this afternoon and they made us go to his place. When we got there, we found Mr. McCloud in his ranch house. He's alive, but recovering from a bad gunshot wound in the back."

"The boss told me he and Cutler were ambushed in a set-up by Tyler and Toby. They killed Cutler and left McCloud for dead. He wrote out in his own writing that he wants Rivers to get the twins and Suella off the place. He says she is meaner than the boys and it was probably her idea."

Hesler was interrupted with an outpouring of anger from the men. They highly respected McCloud and Cutler was a friend to all of them.

"Wait a minute," Hesler said. "I know how you feel. I feel the same way. But this is how the boss wants it to be handled."

"We don't need no outsiders settlin our problems," a voice said from the crowd.

"Well, Rivers ain't exactly no outsider. The boss said Rivers was his son," Hesler added.

"Hesler is telling the truth," Rivers said. "I appreciate the respect you have for Matthew McCloud and I understand how you must feel about your foreman's murder. I'm about as used to having a father as McCloud is to having a son. This is new territory for both of us. I've always roped my own broncs. Now that I know who my father is, his trouble is mine. Especially when the twins plan was to lay the blame for all this on me. I'm gonna handle it. The reason we are here is I didn't want to fight you men before I get at them boys."

"Ain't gonna be no fight here," someone said.

In a sudden move of bodies Rivers and his men were surrounded, grabbed, and tied. It happened so fast the men could do nothing to keep it from happening.

"My name's Rufus Jenkins," one of the men said. "You can lay the blame for this on me. Somebody get some rope and bring two saddled horses down by the barn. I want four of you men to saddle up and bring a horse and pack horse for the woman. If she opens her mouth about anything, we'll hang her too." He looked at Rivers and his men, and then continued, "Mr. McCloud has been the only law we've had around here. We all have known from when we set foot on this ranch what the price was for certain things. The price for killing another man has always been hanging. McCloud has hung a few over the years. Them boys are going to pay the price."

With that said, the men filed outside with a handful left to guard Rivers and his men. It was quiet for a spell and then they heard it.

"Please don't hang us," one of the boys screamed.

They heard the scuffle of people moving and the crying and begging flowing from the mouths of the boys. It was a pitiful sound, hard for anyone to enjoy.

A few minutes later some of the men came and untied Rivers and his friends. They led them outside to see the twins swinging from a pole extended out of the barn loft. The lantern light showed a sullen and subdued woman setting astride a horse being led out of the yard. She was accompanied by four riders.

Rufus Jenkins walked back to Rivers and said, "You tell the boss what took place here tonight. Tell him we gave her enough money to make it a few days in Santa Fe and sent her there. We want him home. When can we come get him?"

"Give him another two or three days and then send a wagon for him," Rivers said. "As bad as I wanted to take care of this for him, I guess it is better that you did it. I owe you my thanks."

"You don't owe us nothing. We owe you for taking care of the boss," Jenkins said.

34

Four months passed before Rivers heard anything from McCloud. He left the ranch three days after the hangings. McCloud had seemed depressed when Rivers told him of the events on the Bar M. Later McCloud told Rivers he was proud the boys handled it and not him. Rivers saw very little of McCloud in the three days before he left, choosing to be busy away from the ranch house. It was his way of handling McCloud's departure.

The impasse was broken on a Tuesday morning. A Bar M rider galloped into the ranch yard and stepped down to approach Rivers.

"The boss wants to know if you folks will come over to the Bar M on Sunday and eat with us. He's planning a big day. Said to tell you we'll be down by the river. He's going to cook a steer and have the boys grease up the guitars. He told me to tell you he really wanted you and your hands to come," the man said.

"Tell your boss we'll come and we appreciate the invite," Rivers said.

The rider smiled and tipped his hat to Mary. He then turned and rode out.

Rivers and his gang left the Crooked Wind early Sunday morning. They arrived at the site about mid morning. They stopped at the top of a knoll and looked down on the festivities already underway. A number of wagons had been pulled under the shade of the big trees along the river. Logs had been snaked in for people to sit on. Four tables covered with cloths obviously held the food. One group of men were cooking a steer over a big fire. Others were playing music and dancing. It seemed the party was in full swing and it appeared a lot of effort had gone in to planning the day. The Crooked Wind folks rode on down to the party.

Rivers knew the time would come when he and Matthew McCloud would confront each other after McCloud had left the ranch. He was in no rush, but figured a social event would be as good as any for it to happen.

Rivers, sided by Mary, rode up with his men and were greeted by McCloud and some of his hands.

"Get down and enjoy yourselves," McCloud said as he walked up to the new arrivals.

Rivers and his hands stepped down and three of his men took all the horses to tie them.

"Mighty nice of you to have us over," Rivers said as he reached out to shake McCloud's outstretched hand.

It was obvious McCloud had regained a lot of his strength. His grip was strong. It was also obvious he had his mind on something other than Rivers. While he was shaking Rivers hand he had his eyes on Mary. He dropped Rivers hand and stepped over to put his hand on the smiling young lady's shoulder.

"It is especially nice to have a beautiful young woman on the place. Welcome," McCloud said.

"Thank you," Mary replied.

They all followed McCloud and he walked into the busy crowd. The men scattered and took seats on the logs.

Rivers walked aside a short distance with McCloud and broke the silence. "You seem to have recovered from your wound. Are you feeling all right?"

"I'm feeling great. Almost back to where I was before I got shot. I owe you for saving my life. I want you to know how grateful I am," McCloud said looking deep into Rivers eyes.

"I am happy to see you strong. You don't owe me any thanks," Rivers said.

"Rivers, do you mind if I walk off away from this crowd with Mary. I want to show her some of the beauty of this river bottom," McCloud said.

"Go ahead. Keep an eye on her though. She's Indian through and through. She might slit your throat," Rivers said with a chuckle.

McCloud walked over to Mary and took her hand. They walked together down to the river. They sat on a huge rock and talked for well over an hour. Rivers looked their way every now and then and enjoyed seeing the two talking. He was happy inside. McCloud could look at the perfect copy of the woman he fell in love with when he was a young man.

The cry went out to come and eat and it brought everybody to the tables, including McCloud and Mary. He removed his hat and with a loud voice prayed, thanking God for the food and visiting neighbors. Afterwards everybody grabbed a plate and enjoyed the feast.

Rivers sat with his friends. Mary sat with McCloud at one of the tables. Rivers enjoyed seeing his men having a good time. They didn't get to do anything like this often.

Afterwards, the music started back up and people sat in small groups visiting and talking. About mid-afternoon Rivers signaled for his men to gather the horses. They needed to get back before dark. He had left three men with the place and he wanted to be there to help them if they needed a hand.

One of the cooks brought a basket of food for him to take to the men he left behind. It occurred to him that McCloud knew all the right things to do as a gentleman.

Rivers looked around for McCloud and spotted him standing up on some high ground overlooking the party. He walked up and extended his hand. "Thanks for a great day. My men have really enjoyed themselves."

"You're welcome," McCloud said. "I want to ask you a favor. First, I want to thank you for sharing Mary with me. Do you think she might could come over and visit me from time to time?"

"I don't see why not," Rivers said.

"There's something else," McCloud said. "One of these days all this will be yours." McCloud watched a frown spread across his son's face. "I don't want to upset you. I wish there was something I could do to make up for the lost years. I want you to know I would if I could."

Rivers looked into the eyes of McCloud and said, "I don't want anything you have. I have a ranch. I will raise the best horses in the country. People will come great distances to have the joy of owning one."

As Rivers was talking Goldy led his big stallion up to the two men and handed Rivers the reins. He then left the men there talking.

Rivers stepped into the saddle and turned his horse away from McCloud.

As he turned his back, McCloud spoke. "Rivers, will it never be any different?"

"It is already different, or I would not be here," Rivers spoke in a low voice. " Something you must always remember. I am Tse-quo-ni, Cherokee warrior from the high mountains where the sun appears. That will never change. Something else you can know. I have been known as Rivers all my life. My mother gave me the name and I have worn it with pride. From this day I will be known as Rivers McCloud. I will wear the name with honor."

Rivers kicked his horse into motion, waved his men to follow, and rode away from McCloud.

The big man stood watching them leave with eyes filling up and tears streaming down his cheeks. One of his hands walked up to where he was and McCloud quickly wiped the tears away.

"Is everything all right Boss?"

"You know what that young man said to me? Said he was going to have the best horse ranch in the country. You know what. He just might do it," McCloud said.

"I don't know about that," the man said in a comforting tone to McCloud, but McCloud was not listening.

"Look at him," McCloud said. "Look at how he rides that horse."

This novel has been printed on acid free paper.
The typeface is Arial 10 point over 15.5.
▲